LITERALLY

Lucy Keating

HARPER TEEN
An Imprint of HarperCollinsPublishers

This book is dedicated to my brothers:

occasional tormentors,

often saviors,

always heroes

HarperTeen is an imprint of HarperCollins Publishers.

Literally
Copyright © 2017 by Alloy Entertainment

www.epicreads.com

alloyentertainment

Produced by Alloy Entertainment
1325 Avenue of the Americas
New York, NY 10019
www.alloyentertainment.com

Library of Congress Control Number: 2016958062

ISBN 978-0-06-238004-3

Design by Elaine Damasco

17 18 19 20 21   PC/LSCH   10 9 8 7 6 5 4 3 2 1

❖

First Edition

Instinctual Response

IT'S 3:02 P.M. on Sunday afternoon, and I should be cleaning my room. Not because it's particularly dirty—it never is. Not because my parents told me to—they never would. Because my calendar says so—in yellow. Errands and necessary "upkeep" are yellow; homework blue; exercise (running on the Boardwalk, surfing with my dad) purple; appointments (teeth cleaning, haircut at The Hive) are in hot pink; and events like dinner with Ava at Papa's Poke Shop or Nisha's birthday party in Malibu are a bright teal. I call that one my "Friends/Fun" section. There are other categories for other things, but I won't bore you with the details. I'm a very visual person. I get that from my mother. I am also highly organized. I get that from absolutely nobody in my family.

The problem with it being three P.M., when I should be cleaning my room, is that I am not. Instead I am lying on my stomach on the living room floor, staring into the eyes of Napoleon, who, from his place under the wheat-colored sofa, stares back at me with challenging eyes, a lone pair of my underpants hanging out of his mouth.

"Don't do it, Napoleon," I warn.

Napoleon growls.

Ava told me the other day, after Napoleon growled at her, too, that she wasn't offended, because it was an instinctual response. "Sometimes the body reacts in ways we can't help, as a way of letting us know how we're really feeling," she told me. "Like how Nisha turns beet red whenever Ray Woods utters even a partial sentence to her. Or you always sweat in your armpits during exams. Or how I've barfed before almost every flight I've ever taken."

"My armpits don't sweat during exams," I protested, and Ava just smiled. It is very like Ava to say something like that. To dwell, not so much on the fact that something is happening, but rather why it is happening in the first place. She is good at trying to see the other side. For me, it's not so complicated. Things happen or they don't. You make them happen or not. And I consider an unexpected, instinctual response—blushing and sweating and growling—highly inconvenient.

Slowly, I reach a hand toward Napoleon's sofa cave, and his growl becomes a snarl. I withdraw my hand with an eye roll that I like to believe he can understand.

Napoleon is my father's dog. He is also my mortal enemy. It's not that I don't like dogs. Those golden retrievers you see lying by the fire in a soup commercial, for example, doing nothing but wagging their tails. Or that bulldog who rides a skateboard, wearing sunglasses, his tongue flapping in the wind. But Napoleon is different. My father found Napoleon in an alley with a dead rat when he was only a few months old. "Poor guy," he said. "Living in conditions like that." But I know the truth. I know that Napoleon challenged that rat to a fight to the death, and Napoleon won.

The back door to the kitchen opens and in wanders my mother, iPad directly in front of her face as she walks, her bob of straight blond hair swinging along with her, followed by Jae, her new design intern. At least I assume it's Jae. I can't see his face behind the giant stack of rolled-up pieces of vellum paper, probably displaying the plans for another one of her beautiful Southern California homes. Mom's specialty is remodeling old bungalows. She has a reputation for simplifying a house's design, modernizing it just enough, but without losing the character of the place. With deep oak floors and heavy beams balanced by bright white walls and mid-century furniture, our house is one of her best advertisements. One of the exotic pillows she sourced from India is currently wedged under my elbows.

"What are you doing on the floor?" my mom asks, still staring at her iPad as she sets down her bag and motions Jae to drop the plans on the counter. Then she grabs two seltzers from the fridge and hands one to him.

"Napoleon has my underpants," I explain.

"What a little pervert," she replies.

Jae just smiles politely. "Hi, Annabelle."

"Hey, Jae," I say, and then I sigh. I want to ask my mother if she could maybe refrain from calling our dog a pervert in front of her intern to whom I have never spoken more than four words on one individual occasion, but I know there's no use. My mother is unconcerned with formalities.

"How do you plan to get them back?" she asks now, finally setting the iPad down and looking over at me.

"Murder him," I say definitively, and she snorts. I glance back at Napoleon. He has not moved a muscle.

"You're a monster," I whisper.

"I'll pretend I didn't hear that," my father says as he strolls into the kitchen, his salt-and-pepper hair in its usual bed-head state, his jeans rolled round the ankles. Nobody ever hears him coming because he is consistently barefoot. "That's the beauty of working from home," he'll say if you point this out.

There's a joke in there, if you know where to look. The joke is that my dad hasn't "worked" in years. He was a TV writer in the late 1990s before selling a big ensemble comedy to a major network, and, after the finale in 2006, hasn't been to an office

4

since. He spends most mornings surfing, which he took up after retirement, and reading, which he's always done. There's a smaller guest house behind our house that my dad refers to as his "lair," where he reads, screens movies, and takes an occasional meeting. Lately, he's been spending more time out there than usual, and occasionally, I've noticed him coming out early in the morning. He must be onto a new idea.

"Should we take a drive?" he asks the room. I notice how wrinkly his T-shirt is. "Head up to Topanga State Beach, maybe grab an early dinner and watch the sunset? What do you say, *you*?"

The *you* is always directed to *me*. I know it's kind of weird, like my own father can't remember my name, but it's actually the opposite. Something about the way he says it makes me feel like I am the only *you* there is. And that makes me feel good.

"I have plans," I explain. "Is that the T-shirt you were wearing yesterday?"

"Forgive me!" my father exclaims, ignoring my question. "What's on deck?"

I steel myself for a moment, considering that maybe if I talk really fast, they won't make fun of me, and we can be done with this conversation. "Well, I have to clean my room and then I have to take a run and—"

My father shoots a glance at my mother, like *How did we create this?* "Maybe you should shake things up a little bit? Prove to yourself that the world isn't going to end if you don't clean your room this afternoon?"

I frown, contemplating his suggestion.

"What are you doing on the floor?" my brother, Sam, says as he bustles into the kitchen, grabbing an apple and taking a giant bite. "Did Napoleon steal your socks again?" he manages through muffled chews.

"Underpants," my mother explains.

"You wanna go for a drive?" my father asks Sam. "Make a day of it? The whole family is coming."

"I'm not available," I say loudly. Why is it so hard for them to understand that even though they prefer to thwart general structure in their own lives, that's not the way I choose to live?

"Right." Sam rolls his eyes. "Maybe in between cleaning your room and taking a run you could find time to remove the giant stick from your—"

"Sam," my father warns. But you can tell he finds it funny.

I am just about to lose my temper when Napoleon makes a break for it, his scraggly body darting out from under the couch and through the kitchen door, which Sam just left wide open.

"Catch him!" I cry, but nobody even pretends to move. I scramble out after Napoleon and into the yard, but I've lost his trail. I am just kneeling down to look under a hydrangea bush, insincerely cooing his name, when I hear it.

"Looking for these?" a voice says, all crackly with just a hint of smirk. I cringe, knowing to whom the voice belongs, then turn slowly to find Elliot Apfel standing in the middle of my lawn, a paper-thin T-shirt falling over his sinewy shoulders, an unreadable expression on his lightly freckled face, my thankfully clean underpants dangling between the thumb and forefinger of his right hand. In his left, squirming like a mutant piglet, is Napoleon.

"Yes," I mutter, feeling myself blush as I snatch them away, and getting more frustrated when I remember what Ava said. Then I think, if there was literally one person on this entire planet I would hope to never be standing on my front lawn holding my underpants, it's Elliot. He will never let me live this down.

"Hot pink?" I hear him say behind me as I turn back to the house.

"Must you comment?" I call out without stopping.

"Did you really expect me not to?" I hear him call back.

Elliot is my brother's best friend. He used to be mine, too, back when we were little. We're the same age. Our moms went to art school together, before they diverged into photography and architecture. But then Elliot hit puberty and started acting weird and also, frankly, rude. And then he got a girlfriend and then another . . . and then another. Elliot has had more girlfriends than I have organizational colors on my calendar, which has always totally boggled my mind, since I don't think he's ever even heard of shampoo.

Now he has Clara, and she has lasted longer than most. Clara is the lead singer of Look at Me, Look at Me, the band that Elliot and Sam started together, the reason Sam states for why he decided to postpone college. I'm nearly one hundred percent certain the real reason is surfing, and I wonder if my parents know this, too. I wonder if, like me, they know it's unlikely that Sam will go to college at all.

Back in the kitchen, my family is still standing around chatting, more like roommates than humans who share genes.

"Elliot!" My dad points a finger enthusiastically. "I bet *you* wanna go for a drive."

"We can't actually, Dad," Sam cuts in. "We have rehearsal. I totally forgot." He turns to Elliot. "Sorry."

Elliot shoves his hands in his pockets. "We're gonna have to postpone rehearsal for a while, actually . . . considering Clara quit the band this afternoon." He purses his lips.

To know Clara Bernard is to know her Instagram. The entirety of my knowledge of her I've gleaned from there. Since she's usually taking selfies or keeping her lips suctioned to Elliot's face, it's difficult to glean her true essence. But her Instagram is well curated. Lots of well-lit, California-girl pictures of her on the beach, or leaning against one of the vintage cars at Elliot's dad's shop, her dark brown hair falling out of some floppy brimmed hat, or writing lyrics moodily in a notebook. The only thing Clara loves more than her Instagram is her boyfriend. At least that's what I always thought.

"She quit?" Sam asks, his eyes wide.

Elliot shrugs. "Apparently, the girl half of He/She got laryngitis and they asked her to fill in."

"Well, she'll be back," Sam says a little frantically, running a hand through his thick hair. Sam has my dad's hair, dark brown and prone to sticking out in wild directions, and I have my mom's. So blonde it's not even California; it's more like snow queen. "I mean, we're all in this together." Sam's voice is slowly increasing in tone and volume as he waits for Elliot to reply. "That's the plan. And she has *you*." He motions to Elliot, and the *you* is an actual squeak. "She'd never give up on you."

For a split second, a shadow flashes across Elliot's unreadable expression. Then he swallows. "Clara and I broke up," he says.

Nobody seems to know how to respond to this statement. Everyone just watches Elliot as he nods his head repeatedly, as it to say *Yes, it's true* to our unspoken questions. Even if I can't stand him, even if he did knock a glass of water onto my laptop while skateboarding through our house a month ago, and call me an embarrassing nickname in front of the captain of the water polo team last Thursday, I have to admit I feel the tiniest bit bad for him. He may never wash his T-shirts and Clara may have the depth of a wading pool, but somehow they worked. Not to mention they're an unnervingly good-looking couple. Were. Past tense.

Elliot exhales then, and I look down, realizing I'm still holding my underpants.

2

The Good Coffees

I OPEN my eyes, like I do every morning, to the impression that palm trees are spying on me. They lean toward the second floor of our house, all gangly and awkward, big, bushy heads tipped as though they are peering into my room.

When people think of Los Angeles, they think sprawl, and they think traffic. Or mansions in Beverly Hills, hidden by ivy-colored walls and accented with sparkling black sports cars in the driveways.

That's usually because they've never been to where we live: Venice. Not the one in Italy, with the canals and the drowning palazzos. My Venice has sweet little bungalows, fences lined with brightly colored bushes, vintage cars that have survived in the easy California weather, and guys riding bikes with surfboards clutched under one arm. I haven't been everywhere, but I'm pretty sure there aren't many places like this, and I love it here. I've been told on more than one occasion that I can be a little uptight, and I like to think that Venice balances me out.

Our house, though, is particularly special. It's an original Craftsman from the days when the neighborhood was just being built. But it's two stories, which is rare, my mom says. It's a corner lot, making it a real presence on our street. My room is right on a corner, so I get all the magic morning light.

My parents bought the place twenty years ago, when Venice was mostly made up of artists and bohemians and a lot of people who lived out of their vans. There's a campaign around these days called Keep Venice Weird. Old shacks are being turned into three-million-dollar moderns. An incense shop on Abbot Kinney was just turned into an artisanal donut bakery. You can't find a coffee for under five dollars. People are afraid we're losing our edge.

When I come downstairs for breakfast, my family is crowded around the dining room table, leaning over the Arts section of the *Los Angeles Times*. Someone has picked up coffee from the expensive new place on Electric Avenue, which means we are either celebrating good news or receiving bad. When I get a closer look at the paper, I see a picture of our house, smack in the middle of the front page.

"I didn't know it would be on the front page!" I exclaim.

"Of course it's on the front page," my dad says, putting a hand somewhere between my mom's shoulder and the lower part of her neck. "It's exactly where it should be." My mom gives a tight smile, and a funny feeling bubbles up through my chest. They used to act this way all the time. A hand on a shoulder, someone's feet propped on someone else's lap while they watched a movie. But I haven't seen it in a while.

A couple months ago a woman named Mathilda Forsythe showed up at our front door. Mathilda was doing an article on The House, my mom explained, for the *LA Times*. She spent the afternoon trolling the floors and examining all the surfaces, asking details about where things were *sourced* and what was *sustainable*, jotting notes down in a Moleskine. Then she returned the next day with a beefy, man-bunned photographer named Silas who took a few shots of the family on the deep-blue couch in the living room, and one with my mother out on the porch, her arm resting along the railing, a smile on her face that said, *Yeah, I got this.*

"This is so cool," I say now. "We have to get it framed! So meta to have an article of your house *in* your house." I'm making a joke, the kind of joke we usually like, but nobody laughs, and immediately, I catch a look between my parents. My brother, too, seems to be in on whatever I am missing.

"What?" I ask.

"Here," my dad says, pushing the coffee cup in my direction

across the table. "I got your favorite; I even remembered to add the cinnamon."

I do not make one move toward the coffee, even though it smells amazing. I now understand that these coffees are not good-news coffees. They are deceitful ones. "What's going on?" I ask again.

"Maybe now isn't the best time," my father starts, but my mother stops him, her voice low but still perfectly clear to me.

"We have to, Ezra. She will hate us more later if we don't tell her now."

I do hate secrets. I hate ambiguity. I don't like to wonder; I need to know. I consider reminding them of this, but the fear creeping up my throat is preventing me from doing very much.

"Your mother and I have been doing some thinking," my dad says. "About our life here. We think it may be time for a change." He stops for a second, and I can see he is really struggling to get the words out. My mom jumps in.

"We'd been mulling it over, and now with this article coming out, Dad talked to Aunt Sandy, and she said this is the perfect time."

I squint at them, trying to read them better. "What are you telling me exactly?"

"They're selling the house, AB," Sam cuts in impatiently.

My mom sighs, and my father puts a hand over his eyes. "Thank you, Sam," he says.

I shake my head. "Why would you do that? This is our home.

And"—I jab a finger down on the *Times* article—"it's famous! Why would you want to sell a house that is famous?"

A strange silence falls over the entire table. Nobody is jumping in for anybody. Neither of my parents says a word. Not even Sam pipes up.

"Aunt Sandy is a real estate agent in Florida," I push. "What does she know?" Why does it feel like nobody is ever paying attention? Like I have to teach them how things work?

"I told you this wasn't the best time," my father says softly. "I told you she would have more questions."

"Then when was, Ezra?" my mother asks curtly. "When two moving trucks pull up?"

Now my father looks at her in a way I've actually never seen. Like he barely knows her. It scares me, and I get the feeling this is not about the house at all. There is something bigger happening here. Maybe it's been something I've been feeling for a while.

"Why would there be two moving trucks?" I ask, and it comes out in a whisper.

My father clenches his jaw, and then he says it all in one breath: "Your mom and I have decided it would make sense to live apart for a while. We really didn't want to tell you this part now. We wanted to tell you about the house, in case any real estate agents show up this week. It wasn't supposed to go like this."

I look at Sam. "Did you know?"

Sam won't look at me. Instead, he looks angrily at my dad. "I told you guys I should tell her." Then he looks down at his plate. "I didn't want to keep this from you, AB."

I feel as though my world is spinning, the breakfast table tipping upside down, like I am falling down a rabbit hole. I put my hands over my eyes to steady myself. I don't understand how this is happening. This is our family. This is our home. This is how it works.

"I am sure you are very upset, but I promise you once you go off to Columbia, your life is going to change so much, you'll hardly even be here," my dad explains, as if I need reminding that soon I will be moving across the entire country for college, away from everything and everyone I know.

"The point is that my life *will* change so much, and I will *need* this to come home to," I say, my voice cracking as I struggle to hold back tears. I do not like this at all. I do not like being displaced. I do not like a disruption in the way things are.

"Well, unfortunately, honey, you don't get to decide," my mother says. I hate when she uses that tone with me. Like she empathizes, when really she doesn't. I hate it especially because she always uses it when she's actually right. "This is for your father and I to decide, and believe me, it has been devastating. But this is what needs to happen. And you're just going to have to try to understand."

I want to argue with her. To make some kind of threat, some

ultimatum. But the scariest part is, I can't. I don't get to decide if they're married or living together or whatever. There is nothing to say. And then my mother sniffs, and I realize she doesn't want to fight about this any more than I do.

"Um, hey," a voice says quietly, and Elliot is there in the doorway. Why is he forever showing up when I don't want him to? He gives a swift knock against the wall. "Sorry to interrupt. . . ."

Sam sighs. "It's okay, man. What's up?"

Elliot throws a quick glance over at me. "Um, I brought back that AUX cable you lent me last night for my car. Thought I'd drop it on my way to school." He puts the cord on the table and starts to back away. "Sorry to interrupt," he says again.

I am staring at the article, clenching my teeth, when I hear my father say it.

"Elliot," he calls just as Elliot is almost at the door and swinging his car keys around his right hand, "would you mind taking Annabelle to school today?"

"Sure." Elliot looks confused as he glances back and forth between my dad and me.

"We can talk more later," my dad tells me, trying to put a hand over mine. But I pull away. To Elliot he says, "Thanks, E. And it looks like we've got an extra coffee from Electric Café, if you're interested."

And then, just like that, my own father hands Elliot Apfel my latte.

"If you're going to drive these beautiful cars, you should really make more of an effort to keep them clean," I observe, crossing one white jean leg over the other and brushing all the sand off the sides. Elliot's dad owns a vintage mechanic shop over on Lincoln Boulevard, where all the big movie prop designers go when they're hired on a period drama. If he doesn't have it, he can get it, is what he always says.

Elliot and I are cruising along Lincoln Boulevard on our way from Venice to school in Santa Monica. I know I'm in a foul mood. My world is being turned upside down. I keep thinking about what my dad said about "living apart." What does that really mean? It sounds temporary. But selling The House? That sounds so . . . final. I sigh out the window, and Elliot doesn't respond; he just keeps driving, a serene look stitched to his face. I have no idea why he's being so calm, but I feel bad, so I mumble, "I love this song."

"Hot pink?" is all Elliot says back, and I regret being nice immediately.

"Mention my underwear again and I will take a baseball bat to your windshield," I say coolly, examining my hair in the passenger mirror. "And on a BMW this rare, it'll cost you upward of two grand."

Elliot snorts. "It's so weird how you care so much about cars."

"Why is it weird?" I ask, rearranging some things in my book bag. Everything in its proper place.

"Because you guys drive your cars into the ground. My dad's always having to pick up one of your parents stranded on the road when whatever beat-up car they're driving finally bites the dust. He says they couldn't tell the difference between a Mazda and a Mercedes."

"And what's your point?"

"My point is, where did you come from?" Elliot asks.

I shrug. "Cars are beautiful. A perfect mix of form and function. When done right, which they haven't been since, like, the 1980s."

Elliot's father's shop has everything from a 1960s VW Beetle to a 1972 Volvo hatchback. And when a car has been sitting around a little too long, like the sparkling white convertible we're currently sitting in, Elliot gets to drive it. As long as when he stops to park it, he puts a little FOR SALE sign on the dash. Like at school, or in front of the coffee shop he hits every morning on his way back from surfing.

"So wait a minute, back it up. You like Paper Girl?" Elliot asks, referring to the music coming out of his speakers, and his whole expression changes from smug to utter surprise. "*You.* Like Paper Girl?" He has one hand on the wheel and an elbow propped up on the window. He angles his head down and toward me like it takes that much effort to believe what I'm saying.

"I can like Paper Girl," I say. "You aren't the only one who is allowed to like them. You don't need a membership card to

18

Slackers Anonymous to appreciate good music." On the east side of Lincoln, we pass our sixth donut shop thus far. I always keep count. LA has more seedy donut shops than it has gas stations. Sam says they are probably drug fronts, but what does he know?

"You're a real piece of work this morning," Elliot observes, eyes still on the road.

"You always are," I shoot back.

We pull up next to a woman in a sparkling black Lexus coup. In the passenger seat, a white cotton ball with two beady eyes and a pink bow in its hair has its paws up on the window, and it stares at Elliot intently.

"What's wrong, Bellybutton?" Elliot coos. Bellybutton is a name he came up with for me when we were younger, and he insists on continuing to use it as a means of torture. "You get a ninety-nine point five out of one hundred on something?"

I laugh, because absolutely not. "For your information, I do have problems. My parents are probably getting divorced, and they are selling The House." I lean down and pick at the seam of my jeans. "And the sand in your car is ruining my outfit."

"That's rough," Elliot says, turning into the school parking lot. "Sam told me last night. I love your parents. They're more my parents than . . . my parents. And that's definitely true of your house."

Elliot and his dad live in an apartment closer to the beach. It's not shabby; it just lacks a certain warmth to it, since neither of them are ever home. More often than not Elliot can be found making breakfast in our kitchen, or playing drums in the garage. Or just lying on the couch in my room uninvited when my brother is late getting home, telling stupid stories when I'm trying to finish a problem set, getting Cheeto dust everywhere.

"So that's it?" I ask. "That's all you've got? My entire childhood existence is circling around the drain, and *that's rough*?"

Elliot pulls into a spot and turns, his syrupy-brown eyes boring into me. "Life is rough sometimes, Bellybutton. Not for you, usually, but for the rest of us."

"Oh, *please*," I say.

His tone is patronizing, like he's messing around, but there's truth behind it. Elliot's parents got divorced when he was young, and then his dad threw himself into his business. To spend any time with him at all, Elliot works part-time at the shop, while his mom lives on some artists' commune in Hawaii. My mom says that's why he's so volatile. Life hasn't been fair to him.

But right now I don't want to think about Elliot's problems. I have my own.

"Whatever. Thanks for the ride, I guess." I smooth my hair and go to put my hand on the door.

"Hey, Annabelle?" Elliot says, and when I turn back he's not looking at me, he's leaning down to grab his phone from under the dash. "Don't worry about the sand. Trust me." I am just about to turn away again, but the next thing he says stops me. "In those jeans, nobody's looking at the sand." He glances up, his eyes meeting mine, and holds it. Elliot has this way of smiling even when he's not, giving the impression that he's all mischief all the time. He uses it on female authority figures, on waitresses, on girls he's hitting on . . . and on me right now.

I wrinkle my nose. Because he's kidding, right? Elliot doesn't compliment my jeans. Elliot grabs the apple off my tray at lunch and keeps walking without a thank-you. He borrows my books because he never buys a copy of his own, and won't return them until I steal the keys to his car. But the longer we sit there, the longer I realize he's not kidding. Then he breaks into a slow smirk, and I can't sit here any longer.

"You're gross," I say, getting out and shutting the door behind me, taking deliberate steps. And I don't look back.

3

Welcome!

SENIOR ARTS Elective is a requirement only a school as hippie-dippie as Cedar Spring would have. Before you graduate you have to pass three classes that *challenge the creative mind specifically.* I took pottery one year, and made a ton of mugs and plates. At least those were useful, utilitarian. Then I did an outdoor sculpture class taught by a visiting teacher where everyone got an easy A. And now I'm stuck with Fiction.

There is more irony in my hatred of creative writing beyond the fact that my father is a successful TV writer. It's that I am actually not that bad at writing, either. I joined the school paper freshman year, and they made me editor in chief by my junior spring. Tell me you want one thousand words on potential bias on the school disciplinary committee, I'm your lady. I can have that for you in three hours. Or I can turn in a piece on what students really think about the new head of school. Or I can go more nuanced, on the pressure of getting in to the right college. I can do words when they are already there, waiting to be grabbed. I can't do words when the story doesn't already exist.

I tried, on the first assignment, to fake it. We were told to write one scene from four different perspectives, and I wrote about having breakfast with my family. But on the page, it was as if all the characters were just robots, staring at one another over their eggs, asking someone to pass the orange juice. I just couldn't imagine the scene from so many angles. How could four people experience one thing that differently?

Miss Epstein suggested that I was hitting too close to home. "Nobody finds our lives more interesting than we do," she said. "Next time, as an exercise, I want you to imagine a story that has nothing to do with your own life. A different character. A different age. A different part of the world. Try your hand at that."

So I tried. And I still did not succeed.

Epstein plows into the classroom now, sheets of paper flying out of her arms, apologizing yet again for being late. A few students who have begun to bank on the extra ten minutes sneak in behind her, and Epstein doesn't even see them. I clasp my hands tightly in my lap, bracing myself for what she'll ask us to do today. A group assignment or, worse, an invitation to read aloud?

Instead, Epstein throws all her papers down on her desk, stabilizing her body with both arms as she leans across it, beaming at us.

"I know we usually spend this time creating, critiquing, editing," she says, straightening up, her right wrist moving in a circular motion as though she's painting her thoughts for us. "But I thought we'd take a little break from that so I could introduce a friend of mine. She's a well-known author in the young adult genre and she's come in today to talk about process, about publishing, and about making a career out of this temperamental beast we call writing. Class, please welcome my dear friend and MFA classmate, Lucy Keating."

A woman appears in the doorway. She's on the taller side, with long, wavy brown hair, red lipstick, and glasses with thick black frames. She's in an immaculate white silk collared shirt tucked into some boyfriend jeans and chic black booties. Over her shoulder is a pale blue leather tote, and she drops it by the desk when she walks in, then turns to look at all of us with an easy smile.

"Hi." Lucy gives a small wave. "I'll keep my intro brief because usually people like to ask questions. I'm Lucy Keating, and I've written six contemporary young adult novels; all but one have been *New York Times* bestsellers. I majored in English at Brown before getting a job at a publisher in New York, writing at night, and eventually convincing them to publish my first novel, *Maybe in Another Life*. Then I did an MFA at Columbia where I met the incredible Ruth Epstein"—she pauses to smile at our teacher—"and I recently moved to LA from New York with a couple of scraggly dogs. I am loving the sunshine, but missing all the mean people." Lucy gives a wry smile and I can see that beneath the charm there is a seriousness about her.

"Looks like we have a question already?" Lucy chuckles, then points to Maya Davis, whose hand is so high up in the air it's like she's trying to touch the ceiling.

"Do you plan on writing a sequel to *Maybe in Another Life*?" Maya asks. She's blushing and stumbling over her words, and I realize: Maya is a fan. And now I remember from where I know Lucy's name. Lucy is the one who writes all those sad, romantic books that always leave my best friend, Ava, in a puddle of tears. A girl and boy who fall hopelessly in love the summer before he's deployed. A boy from the wrong side of the tracks who falls for an unattainable girl, even when her father gets in their way. More movies than I can count on one hand have been made from her books. The posters always show a couple in some kind of dramatic embrace, and usually someone is crying. I find them totally unrealistic and completely ridiculous.

"Maybe some day," Lucy replies, and though her tone is upbeat, I detect a strain in her voice. "I did love those characters, but I got kind of tired of writing those stories. So much sadness." Lucy looks off for a moment, distracted, then blinks.

"Let's just say I only want to write Happy Endings these days. I think my characters deserve that for a change." She casts a glance my way, and a weird feeling takes over my body, but just like that it's gone.

"Can you tell us what you're working on now?" Maya says, leaning forward eagerly over her desk.

Lucy nods, and I start tuning out, staring out the window onto the quad, where Elliot is chatting up some girls during their free period. I would bet two hundred dollars that Elliot does *not* have a free period, though. My thoughts wander back to this morning and his weird comment about my jeans when I hear Lucy start to answer Maya's question.

"I've actually become pretty inspired by my time in LA," she says. "Right now I'm working on a story about a girl who lives in Venice Beach with her parents and older brother."

I find myself turning back toward the room again. This gets my attention.

"Oh, and of course, their weird little dog, who is always causing trouble." Lucy laughs.

The whole class laughs, too, except for me. *Wait* . . .

Lucy continues. "Her life is pretty perfect, everything is very within her control, but she begins to grow up and learn life isn't so simple. For example, not everything is as smooth at home as she thinks."

Now I am leaning over my desk a little bit, too, and squinting at her. My throat feels a little dry.

Lucy sits on the desk and places her hands on her knees. "And speaking of home, her parents are separating—maybe even getting divorced—and they've decided to sell their house. It's a really special place, on one of the walk streets. And she's lived there her whole life, so she's pretty upset about it."

A series of murmurs and thoughtful *Mmmms* rise up from my classmates, while my heart starts to pound in my chest. I look around, frowning. "Is this a joke?" I finally ask out loud.

At this, the whole class falls silent. "Annabelle?" Ms. Epstein asks, more as an accusation than a question. "Why would Lucy joke about her work?"

"S-sorry," I stutter. "It's just that . . . she's describing my life."

In response to this statement, Lucy watches me coolly, her head slightly tilted to one side. It makes me uncomfortable. But Ms. Epstein lets out a giggle, placing a hand on Lucy's shoulder. "That's why she's such a genius! Everyone feels that in some way, she is 'writing their life'!"

Maya's hand shoots up again, and Lucy breaks her stare to give her a casual nod. "And what about the romance?" Maya asks. "Will there be some juicy love story?"

Lucy grins. "What do you think?"

Maya smiles broadly just as someone else appears in the doorway.

This time it's the silhouette of a teenage boy I've never seen before. And the sharp decline in the chatter of my classmates lets me know that I am not the only one who finds him noteworthy. There is something about his face. The way he stands, chin up, shoulders back. Big blue, almond-shaped eyes that smile even though his mouth doesn't. I can't explain it, but it's like he is a star in a movie and we are all just extras.

"Right on time," Lucy says, which strikes me as a little odd, because he isn't on time at all. Then she says more loudly, "Welcome!"

The boy gives a small wave, a slight jerk upward of a hand, and purses his lips. "Hey," he says. "Hi." The second hi is louder, like he's getting his bearings despite being completely on the spot. Then he clears his throat before saying, "I'm Will."

Will. I turn the name over in my brain. Classic. Solid. Cute. Intended to govern a country.

"Oh, right," Epstein chimes in, gently smacking her forehead with her left hand and shuffling through some papers on top of her desk. "Will Hale. I've got you right here." She pulls out a sheet of paper and gives it a once-over. "A transfer halfway through senior year is pretty uncommon."

Will nods. "Yes, ma'am," he says, and I'm surprised by his manners. "Not my decision, of course, but I'm trying to make the best of it."

Epstein smiles, obviously charmed. "Well, go ahead and have a seat." She motions as she fans herself lightly with her papers. "It looks like there's a spot by Annabelle."

No there isn't, I'm about to say. Izzy Ross is sitting next to me. At least she was. But when I look now Izzy isn't there; she's in the far corner, sneaking looks at her phone beneath her desk.

I am so busy looking at Izzy that I don't realize Will has already made his way over. I'm just glancing up when my pen goes flying off my desk, even though my hands were in my lap. What is going on?

Will dutifully crouches down to pick up the pen and hand it back to me, but when his eyes meet mine, they get even wider than they already were.

"Hi" is all he says, blinking a few times, eyes rimmed by thick lashes.

"Hey," I say back, taking the pen. When he doesn't move from the floor, I whisper, "What?"

Will looks a moment longer, and then he shakes his head and clears his throat. "Nothing," he says.

"Then why are you on the floor?" I whisper back. Because why is he?

"Right," Will answers, and attempts to unobtrusively take a seat. Which is nearly impossible to do when you are not only the new kid, but hands down the cutest guy to ever walk the halls of Cedar Spring.

⟡

Lucy Keating is just throwing her tote bag into the backseat of a vintage Volkswagen Beetle when I catch her outside.

"Nice car," I say as I approach.

"Thanks," she says, not the least bit surprised to see me, as though she didn't just plot out my life story for my high school creative writing class.

I pause before I speak again, fully understanding how strange I am about to sound. But I have no choice. This is too weird. "I don't know how or why you are doing it, but I'd really appreciate if you'd stop writing about my life," I say, and swallow.

Lucy lets out small laugh and turns toward me, one hand on the car window and one on her hip. I expect her to tell me I am insane. But she doesn't. "Annabelle," she says, "I'm not writing about you. I am writing *you*."

I blink a few times. "I don't understand," I say.

"You are in my book," Lucy says, as though she's explaining that today is Tuesday. "You're a character. In fact, so is everyone." The hand holding her car keys makes a sweeping motion over the façade of my school.

I stop and look around the parking lot, wishing someone else was here to witness this. I know authors have a reputation for being crazy—too much time spent isolated with only themselves to talk to—but this is a little much.

"Very funny. That could not make less sense," I tell her.

"The funny thing is, it actually does make sense when you think about it," Lucy says. "Some of my characters demand to be heard. Others just sit in a drawer, waiting for the right time." At the look on my face, she tilts her head. "You don't believe me."

"Of course I don't believe you!" I burst out. "What do you expect me to say? *Oh cool, what happens next?*"

30

"That's okay." Lucy shrugs and turns to get in her car. "It doesn't really matter either way."

I am about to argue back when a voice comes over the school loudspeaker. "Will Annabelle Burns please make her way to Dr. Piper's office?" it says.

I sigh. *Piper*. What could *she* possibly want?

"Annabelle Burns to Dr. Piper's office, please," the voice says again.

"Looks like everything is right on track." Lucy winks as she shuts her door and rolls down the window. "Have fun." Then she peels out of the parking lot, leaving me alone and very confused.

4

She Is Not Good with the Boy Stuff

SOMEONE LIKE me shouldn't be used to being summoned to the principal's office at the last minute. Someone like me, with a solid 4.0, killer extracurriculars, and an immaculate disciplinary record, makes appointments and attends those appointments gladly, ready to be told how well they're doing and what an excellent model they are for the rest of the student body. And if it isn't *too* much trouble, would someone like me mind having my photograph taken for the alumni magazine?

That's not exactly the case for me and our head of school, Dr. Piper. It seems that my unwillingness to *fudge the truth*, as she would say, or look past certain *complications* and *small snafus* in the administration, puts a sour taste in Dr. Piper's mouth. "The old editor of the paper," she once patronized me, leaning down from her perch on her desk, her tight sheath dress straining against her large bosom, "knew exactly how to toe the fine line between the truth and . . . and—"

"And *lying*?" I'd asked, and Piper exhaled loudly through her nose, her freshly done hair blowing away from her face in a single curtain of shiny locks.

This is the reason I am so surprised when I walk through the door of her office to see a sickly sweet smile plastered across her cheeks, and not the usual scrutinizing stare.

"Am I early?" I ask.

Dr. Piper shoots a glance to the right of the room, and I scoot in a few more steps to find that we aren't alone. Will, the new guy, is leaning on a bookshelf, clutching a bunch of textbooks to his chest.

"Hi," he says, and clears his throat again.

"Hey," I say before turning back to Dr. Piper in confusion. "Seriously, am I early?" I repeat.

"You're right on time," Piper replies. Why does everyone keep saying that today? "I take it you've already had the pleasure of meeting our newest transfer." She motions a red-taloned hand as though welcoming Will to the stage.

"Sort of." I shrug.

Dr. Piper beams. "I was hoping you could do us a favor, AB," she says. I hate it when she calls me that name, as if we're close. "Our new friend Will needs someone to show him around. Sadie Kim was supposed to do it, but she mysteriously came down with some kind of stomach bug only moments ago, and Will said yours was the only other name on campus he knew. I told him wasn't that convenient, as you're one of my favorite students."

I raise my eyebrows at her like, *Is that so?*

Piper ignores the look. "So what do you say?"

Will gives a wide smile, like *Please?*

I really do not have time for this, I think. But all I end up saying is "Sure. I was just heading to lunch." Then, not knowing what else to say, I exit the office. When Will doesn't follow, I pause in the doorway.

"Should I come?" Will asks, leaning forward curiously.

"Obviously," I reply. I'm not trying to be rude, but I have a ton of articles to assign for the student paper, and oh, yeah, a crazy lady just told me I'm a fictional character, ten minutes ago in the parking lot.

Will's grin grows even wider as he follows.

"I really appreciate this." Will walks quickly to keep up with my pace as we make our way through the halls. His steps are bouncy and confident. All around us other students turn to inspect him as he passes.

"People think you're interesting," I tell him.

"Wait till they find out the *truth*," he says, and when I look at him, he gives me a goofy grin.

"Are you always this happy?" I ask.

"Are you always this direct?" he replies, and this time I smile back.

"Always," I say.

"So what did you think of that class today?" he asks as we exit the administrative building and head across campus. "I thought that author seemed pretty cool."

I groan. "Don't remind me."

"Not a big fan of the written word?" he asks.

"I *love* writing," I tell him, shifting my bag to the side as someone jogs between us on the path. "I'm the editor in chief of our school paper."

"Whoa, that's cool." Will shifts his backpack around and places his phone in the pocket. "How'd you get into that?"

"Diane Sawyer," I answer simply.

Will frowns. "The newscaster? My grandmother loves her. Aren't you a little young to be a *fan* of *Diane*?" He smiles at his own rhyme.

"So?" I ask.

"No, I'm just saying . . ." Will's smile disappears, his eyes going a little wider. "Okay, sorry. Explain to me your love for Diane Sawyer."

"You really want to know?" I ask, genuinely surprised.

"No, I'd rather walk in silence and not learn anything about the one other student I've met today." Will tilts his head and gives me a look.

I laugh in spite of myself. "Okay," I say. "There's not that much to tell." We walk into the student center, the double doors of the dining hall swinging back and forth ahead. "Basically, we watched her interview with Malala Yousafzai in school one day, and while Malala's bravery nearly made my heart stop beating, Diane's ability to bring her story to life made it race. Since then, I've watched every interview I can get my hands on. Hillary Clinton, Caitlin Jenner, even a special on Jackie O. The way she's able to see patterns, to distill the essence of someone's story down to a meaningful message, to ask just the right questions, takes my breath away." We've stopped outside the double doors. "Also, nobody has ever looked fiercer in a crisp white button-down."

Will doesn't say anything; he just looks at me. Then he nods.

"What?" I ask.

"Nothing." Will shakes his head. "You just surprised me, that's all."

I don't know what he means, but I don't really have the time to find out. "You ready for your high school dining hall experience?" I ask instead.

"Ready as I'll ever be," Will replies.

⸰⸰⸰

My friends are The Loud Table in the dining hall. It's where Elliot and Sam got the idea for Look at Me, Look at Me as a band name. That and our society's ever-growing obsession with how we portray ourselves. Facebook, Instagram, Snapchat . . . and whatever comes next.

"Those girls will do anything for attention," Elliot always complains.

"They're my *friends*," I always say back, usually accompanied by a shove.

"Well, they're *annoying*," he teases then, stepping closer. I always walk away in a huff, leaving him chuckling to himself.

Okay, so I do know what he means. My friends tend to take on this weird persona when they know people are looking. Their voices get higher, louder, and they always seem to be standing up at the table instead of sitting at it. They do a lot of *gesticulating*.

Actually, I want to tell them, *we can get just as much of a sense of the cute waiter at Escuela Taqueria who hit on you yesterday without you standing up and shouting it.*

But they would just laugh. "Oh, are we embarrassing you, AB?" Their voices becoming louder, turning into a waterfall of teen shrieks. "ARE WE EMBARASSING YOU, ANNABELLE BURNS?" And I'd cover my ears with my hands and lean over the table, but I'd still be laughing. Sometimes, when you prefer to play things a little under the radar, you recognize the significance of keeping people around who do not.

And yet now, as we approach the table, there is no gesticulating. No raised voices or fits of giggles. They stare at me and Will like a set of bored chickens waiting for their eggs to hatch. Faces expressionless, eyes large, all in a little row.

"Hi, everyone," I say loudly, trying to draw attention to how weird they are being without actually having to say so, and snap them out of whatever they think they are doing.

"Hey, Annabelle . . ." Ava says as we take a seat. Both the slowness of her speech and use of my full name a way of her saying right back *We'll stop being weird when you tell us who the babe is.* Ava and I have been able to communicate borderline telepathically since the third grade.

"Everyone," I say, "this is Will Hale. He just moved here."

"Halfway through senior year?" Nisha says. "That sucks."

I shoot her a look that says, *Cut it out.* Nisha has an attitude problem. But Will just smiles knowingly.

"You'd think, right?" he says with a shrug, grabbing a grape and tossing it in his mouth.

"So, Will Hale, who were you at your old school?" Ava asks, as though this is a job interview.

"Myself?" Will says through grape chews, looking confused.

"No, like, what was your thing? Jock? Band geek? Judging from the clothes I think we can rule out skater punk." Nisha snorts.

Will holds his arms out wide and lets his eyes run over his outfit. He's got on a perfectly worn in chambray shirt, and deep olive khakis. "What's wrong with my clothes?" he asks good-naturedly.

"Nothing," the whole table replies enthusiastically, and I cringe.

"Phew," Will breathes, his eyes sparkling. "Wanna make a good impression." He tilts his head toward me with a smirk, letting his hand rest on my knee just long enough for me to catch my breath. "How am I doing so far?"

"Fine," I squeak.

"Cool," Will says quietly, still gazing into my eyes. I swallow.

"Hello?" Nisha throws a Goldfish across the table and it nails me on the nose. I shoot her a fiery stare, but if she notices, she ignores it. "Will didn't answer our question."

"I was a little bit of everything." Will shrugs.

"A Little Bit of Everything is a title many strive for, but few actually accomplish," Ava states. "Prove it."

Will sighs. "Well, I was cocaptain of the soccer team, president of the Debate Club . . ."

"Duh and duh," Ava says as she sips Diet Coke through a straw.

"Hosted my own radio show, head of the Wilderness Outing Club—"

"Impressive, but not entirely surprising," Nisha says to Ava, as though they are two scientists observing an animal in the wild.

". . . and a four-year member of the Mathletes," Will finishes.

The table goes quiet. Now my friends are looking at Will like he is a woolly mammoth someone just uncovered on the tundra.

"Seriously?" Nisha says.

"No instruments?" Ava finally asks.

"Ah, you've found my weakness." Will points a finger at her. "Terrible at all of them, and don't think I didn't try. I love music; I just can't actively participate in it."

"That's okay, neither can I," I tell him, surprising myself when I let my own hand pat his knee. The look on Will's face says he is thrilled.

"Okay, you've convinced us," Ava announces. "With those credentials, I am confident you'll be able to survive this crazy institution after all."

"So far it doesn't seem that bad," Will says. I look at my friends and see they are looking at me, all googly-eyed, and then realize that Will has been smiling at me all along.

"Oh," I say, feeling myself blush.

"She is not good with the boy stuff," Nisha whispers to Ava, and Ava snorts her Diet Coke.

Of course, like on so many occasions, I walk out of class at the end of the school day having no idea who is picking me up. They swap in and out a lot. Most of the time it's Dad, but sometimes Mom, if she has a meeting over on this side of town, or maybe Sam or, on rare occasions, one of Mom's interns. But this time Elliot is there, waiting.

He's leaning against the back of the BMW with a smug expression on his face, his long legs crossed at the ankles and his arms crossed, too, each hand gripping an opposite bicep.

I know that, though I can't see them, his drumsticks are probably sticking out of his back pocket. He thinks he's so cool. A real redheaded James Dean.

"You look lost," Elliot observes when I am just a few car lengths away, and I stop and make a face at him.

"Since when do you care?" I ask. I want to hear him say it. Hear him ask, "Annabelle, do you need a ride?" Because it's just so like him not to. To let other people do the heavy lifting in favor of an ever-present air of Who Gives a Crap?

But Elliot doesn't reply; he just keeps smiling, maybe a little wider this time, because the trouble is he wants me to ask him back. Because we are playing a game here. Because he knows I don't have a choice. It's this or I walk. And I am just about to do exactly that when Will's perfect silhouette comes into view between us.

"Annabelle!" he says loudly, maybe nervously. "Hey. Hi." I like the way he does that. The two hellos, as if he's not sure which one sounds better, so he's giving them both a shot.

"Hey, Will," I say, and it comes out in sort of a sigh, and I want to crawl behind one of the cars I'm standing next to. "How was the rest of your first day?"

Behind Will's shiny black hair, I watch one of Elliot's eyebrows rise quizzically.

Will nods. "It was great," he says, "thanks to my tour guide."

Both Elliot's eyebrows are now raised.

I giggle, feeling my face flush a little. "I did nothing," I say.

And then I say, "What?" Because he's looking at me again, in that way. That way like I've got something in my teeth.

Will dips his head down like a nervous little kid, and scuffs one of his feet on the pavement. Then he looks up. "I was just thinking. Would you like a ride home?"

Now both Elliot's eyebrows are knitted together in a squinty, confused frown, like he did not plan for this and possibly like Will is speaking another language.

Will sees me looking behind him, and I am instantly nervous that he's going to assume Elliot is my boyfriend. My annoying delinquent boyfriend, and maybe he'll think I'm not available anymore. But instead he just says, as kindly as he's been to everyone else today, "Oh, hey, man. I'm Will."

"Elliot" is all Elliot says, without extending a hand.

"Okay!" I say, grabbing Will by the arm, because Elliot is not going to ruin this for me. Tell some annoying joke about my childhood or give me a noogie. "A ride would actually be great," I tell him as we walk away. "My family bailed on me and *nobody else offered*," I say the last part loudly, so certain parties will hear. And as we peel out of the parking lot in Will's car, certain parties are still leaning, still staring, still frowning.

Will's car is cleaner than my house looks when my grandmother comes to visit. Which is amazing, since he has a surfboard on the top of his hatchback.

"Is the surfboard just for show?" I ask as we pull onto Ocean Boulevard.

"What?" Will says as he finishes putting my address into his GPS. "No way. I'm from Hawaii. My grandfather taught me as soon as I learned to swim. I go almost every morning. At least I used to, before we moved here."

"I didn't mean to assume," I explain. More often than not, I have to apologize after asking a question. My dad says my tone can be a little abrupt. "Just most of the guys I know who surf a lot tend to bring the beach home with them." Without even realizing it, I reach down and run my hand along the seam of my jeans again, searching for stray pieces of sand from Elliot's car.

Will shrugs, looking embarrassed. "Not very cool, huh," he says. "I'm kind of a clean freak. Check it out." He flips down the sun shield to reveal a clear sheet of pockets for all the necessities: gum, Advil, an extra USB cable, gas card, quarters. "Lame, huh?"

But I am in awe of the organization. Everything in its proper place. "Where can I get one?" I breathe.

Will makes a small groaning noise. "I wish you hadn't asked that," he says.

"Why?" I ask, and I can't help smiling every time I look at him.

"Because I made it myself," he mutters, as though maybe if I don't hear him I won't ask him to repeat himself.

My mouth falls open a little bit. "You made your own car organizer?" I ask.

Will shrugs. "Well, I really just like when there is a spot for everything. I went to, like, six hardware stores and auto shops, and nobody had what I wanted, so yeah . . . I made it." Again, his tone drops off at the end of the sentence.

I reach up and run my hand over the sleeve. It's absolutely perfect. "You're perfect," I tell him. "I mean—" I straighten up and try again. "You're perfect. *I mean*"—I put a hand over my face, shaking my head—*"it's perfect."*

Will is laughing and blushing, too, and deep in the center of my rib cage, something flutters. The car smells a little bit woody, but also a little bit sweet.

"So where's the pocket for the air freshener?" I ask curiously, thinking maybe I'll get one for myself. And put it on my pillow at night.

Will looks confused. "I don't buy those." He wrinkles a nose. "They make me kinda nauseous. What, is that a hint?"

"Then what smells so good in here?" I say before I can stop myself, before realizing it's probably just him.

"Is this it?" Will politely dodges my question, and I realize we're already outside my house. Where did the time go? "Your house is cool," he says, leaning forward across my seat to look out the window. The closer he gets, the sweeter it gets. Yes, it's definitely him. I swallow. And suddenly I want to lay a hand against his perfect olive-skinned cheek, but then I remember we just met five hours ago.

"Sensitive subject at the moment," I say instead. "My parents are selling it."

"Been there," Will says. "Doesn't feel great, does it?" He's looking at me so intently, his entire body facing me. Not like I happen to be where he is. Like I am where he wants to be. I remember Ava telling me about an article she read on body language that stated if a guy's body faces toward you, even his shoes, he probably likes you. At the time it didn't mean very much to me, since I hadn't spent enough time around any guys to notice. But now I am noticing.

"They told me this morning." I sigh. Then, even though I just met him, I add, "And they told me they are separating." I don't want to look at Will, so I look to the right, but that only forces me to stare at The House, my world, ready to fall apart. So I look up. The sky is strangely gray, considering how sunny it was only an hour earlier. Then I feel a hand on my shoulder.

"I'm sorry," Will says. "I don't know what to say, except . . . that really does suck." He gives me a squeeze, and it tingles.

"Thanks" is all I can say back, and something sits between us.

"Will you go out with me?" Will says suddenly, and my mouth almost falls open.

"Um," I say.

"I know you don't know me very well," Will continues. "I know I'm supposed to get to know you a little better and then maybe pretend I don't like you or something, and then ask you out as soon as you get jealous. But I hate games, and ambiguity makes me nervous. I think I *already* like you. And I think once you get to know me better, you might feel the same about me."

"I . . ." is all I say. Because really?

"I know it's kind of last minute," Will presses on, "but there's a show tomorrow night. You said you like music, and this band I'm pretty obsessed with is playing."

My face is on fire, and I look down at my hands, because I don't have a lot of experience with this. I've never been asked out on a date before. I've never even really been asked out on ambiguous hangouts.

"What band?" is all I can manage to get out. Then even more nervousness piles up in my belly. What if it's something awful? Could I really date a guy with poor taste in music?

"Not sure if you've heard of them, but they're called Paper Girl. I promise, they're amazing."

My eyes jerk in Will's direction. "I love Paper Girl," I whisper.

Will's head pulls back in surprise, the corner of his mouth turning up. "Seriously?" he asks.

"Seriously." I nod. Suddenly, I can't take my eyes off his face. The silence is broken by a noise on the windshield. I jump.

"It's just rain." Will laughs.

"What's rain?" I ask. "This is Los Angeles!"

"Good point," he says. "Do you have a raincoat?"

"This is Los Angeles!" I say again. And Will just throws his head back and laughs.

"Okay, let me help you," he says.

"I'll be fine," I assure him, and am just about to get out, when it starts coming down hard. I duck back in quickly. "This is so weird!" I exclaim. "I can't remember the last time it rained like this."

But Will isn't listening. Before I can stop him, he's out of the car, dashing around to my side, an athletic jacket held over his head. He opens my door and pulls me out under his warm, heavy boy arm, under the umbrella of his coat, and we run to The House, me squealing the whole way.

Once we're shrouded by the canopy of our front stoop, Will looks down at me with a smirk, his eyes sparkling as he shakes the wetness out of his hair. "This was fun," he says, his voice is low. Then he pulls the jacket down from his arms and wraps it snugly around my shoulders. "Looking forward to tomorrow night. And thanks again for today. Stay dry." And just like that he's gone, dashing back out to the car through the rain, my knight in shining armor. But suddenly, he stops.

"Hey, Annabelle!" he calls out, squinting through the rain.

"Yeah?" I yell back.

"You never actually answered my question." He grins, even though he's soaked.

I start giggling. I can't help it. "Yes, Will Hale, I will go out with you!" I exclaim, and when he does a fist pump, I laugh harder.

When I walk through the kitchen, I know where Napoleon is by the low growl that comes out from below the kitchen table. Sometimes my mom gives him the dry end of a loaf of French bread, and he takes it under there like a tiny wolf in his cave. We call them Bread Bones.

"Good afternoon to you, too," I mutter.

My mother is at the center island with Jae, drinking tea and reviewing some blueprints.

"Is it my imagination or did you get picked up by one cute guy today and returned by another?" she asks. But I just wrap Will's jacket around my shoulders and head upstairs with a smile.

5

What's Breaking Your Heart Tonight?

MY DAD taught me a long time ago that a run would calm me down. He walked into my room one Saturday afternoon and found me rearranging my bookshelf, stacks and stacks surrounding me like building blocks.

"Didn't you just do this a month ago?" he asked.

I paused. "That was by genre," I explained. "This time it's by color."

"Come with me," he said, turning around and walking back out my bedroom door. "But first put on gym clothes."

My dad gets it because he's that way, too. A little intense. But you'd never know, because every morning he gets up and does something. Maybe it's a run; maybe it's surfing. But he works it all out so he can get down to what matters. And yeah, maybe he doesn't have a lot on his schedule, so to speak, but he's always in a good mood, and he's always there to listen. Or he was. Who knows where he will be after they separate?

Now I run almost every day in the late afternoon or evening, just before dusk. When I run, I can't think about the homework I still have to do or the articles I have to finish for the school paper, because there's no way I could possibly do them at this moment, two miles away on the beach in Santa Monica, dodging people on bikes and dogs of all sizes on leashes. And it's exactly when I get to that place, when I start making the jog from Main Street down to the Boardwalk, the ocean waiting up ahead, palm tree silhouettes cutting into the sky, that's when I really get going. When I feel like a bird that's broken through the net of its sanctuary. That's when I really fly.

Today when my feet hit the pavement, I'm already bouncing with energy. No thanks to the ground, which is as dry and cracked as ever, and once again makes me consider the strangeness of that temporary downpour with Will. But to be honest, I don't really care. Will, with his sweet smell and his chivalry, his heavy arm wrapped around me as he hustled me to my door. Will, grinning at me through the rain.

It's not that I have never had a boyfriend in an official capacity. In the fifth grade, Nisha decided we all needed one. Just like that, like we all needed the newest pair of jeans. We talked about it casually at a sleepover, the idea of boyfriends, and then she just called me up one day and was all, "So what do you think of Teddy Shipman?" And I was like, "He's okay," and she goes, "Well, I called him and asked him if he wanted to go out with you, and he said cool, so I guess it's a thing!" "I guess," I remember mumbling, kind of stunned. The logistics of the arrangement were starting to overwhelm me. What would this mean, exactly? How much of my time would now belong to Teddy? What color should he be in my calendar?

Turns out very little. Turns out Nisha, at the tender age of eleven, knew more about life than any of us did. We didn't have to hang out with boyfriends so much as we had to be able to say we had them. There was an awkward exchange of valentines, a couple group hangs, and that was really all the effort I had to put in. I ended it a few months later when Teddy told someone he wanted to kiss me. I wrote him a polite note saying I felt we were moving too fast. I just wasn't prepared for the intimacy. But it didn't matter; our places were solidified as the coolest girls in the grade from there on out.

What I mean is, I've never had a boyfriend in the practical sense. Nobody saving me a spot in the library, or holding my hand during assembly, or leaving a note on the whiteboard at school before my next class. Having a boyfriend requires so much time. There is so much "being chill" that needs to be done. So much "go with the flow" to be faked. And the games! You are supposed to like someone but not really say so . . . You are supposed to be able to tell when someone wants to kiss you when it hasn't been discussed. There is too much that isn't said. I don't really understand a lot of guys, and they don't seem to understand me. Plus, boys my age don't make advanced plans. They text *What's up?* or *What are you doing now?* and you are expected to be there. Can you imagine what that would do to my schedule?

And so, for this very reason, we can all just imagine what Will "I don't like ambiguity" Hale and his invitation to see Paper Girl are doing to my insides.

On my way home I swing by Rosewood Café & Bookstore, where Ava has her sneakers up on the register. Rosewood never has a lot of customers, but on Tuesday nights it has nobody at all. Ava scored the perfect gig. A few years back when Amazon reimbursed people for some weird tax they'd unfairly charged to every Kindle book you bought, most people got about three dollars. Ava got $342. That's how many books she reads regularly. I read, too, but I read the newspaper and autobiographies of badass women and historical figures. Ava loves romantic fiction. The real, get-in-your-bones, make-your-skin-tingle, make-your-eyes-water kind, she says. I say it's more about girls who love boys they can't have until the boy notices them for some reason they never did before. I say it's all the same. But I don't say it to Ava anymore, because that infuriates her.

Ava is a lover in real life, too. She's had a string of relatively long-term, serious boyfriends, all wildly different, all pretty flawed, all of whom she loves to the very ends of the earth, until one day she decides she just doesn't, and she very politely moves on to another. And none of them ever hate her for it. It's always an amicable breakup. A part of me has always been jealous of the way she can give herself to someone so easily, and accept that love in return.

"What's breaking your heart tonight?" I call out to her, and it takes her a moment to even look up. She's got a hand buried deep in her brown curls, her mouth hanging slightly agape. When she does meet my eyes it's with a glossed-over expression, so I decide to see for myself.

"Something True," I read out loud. *"When Samantha Watson's parents die in a tragic car accident, she moves to a farm in Iowa with her estranged aunt, only to discover that getting back to basics is exactly what her heart needed."* I look up at Ava with mock intrigue. "Let me guess," I say. "A young dairy farmer catches her eye? Just tell me"—I throw my body over the front desk, and Ava rolls her eyes in response—*"will they make it?"*

"You're coldhearted," Ava says. "But I shouldn't be surprised. Every time we tried to play make-believe as kids, you just wanted to be real people who already existed. Like *newscasters.*" She makes a gagging noise.

"This is *WBZN News At Night*—Welcome Home," I say in my best faux newscaster accent, and flash Ava a big grin.

Ava shakes her head, then catches my eye with a more serious look. "Hey. Do you want to talk about it?"

I know what she means. The separation. The House. I texted her about it before first period.

"Not yet," I reply, wandering over to the biography section, and I glance back to see her nodding. She'll be there when I'm ready.

I start to pull the volumes out one by one, then pause.

"Here's something I do want to talk about." I turn back around, leaning against the shelf, crossing my arms over my chest in thought. "I got asked out on a date this afternoon."

As I anticipated, Ava is by my side in an instant.

"Tell me," she says, facing in my direction and leaning her own shoulder against the stacks.

"Tell you what?" I say casually, pulling out another book. As a romantic, this is going to kill her, and I want to draw it out. "Tell you how Will drove me home from school today, and how he just happened to ask me to see my favorite band tomorrow night?" I hold the book in front of my face to examine it, then make a face. *"Paris Hilton: The Untold Story."* Gross.

But Ava doesn't squeal. She is all business, her eyes boring into me. She takes the book from me and snaps it shut, replacing it on the shelf. "I don't have time for games. Tell me all."

I sigh. "I can't believe I'm about to say this, but I think he might be perfect."

I glance over and find Ava's mouth hanging open. "You realize you've never said that about anyone before."

"I know."

"Like, not even Jamie Garcia, when he asked you to prom last year," she says.

"I know." Jamie was our school president, headed to Stanford, and also happened to look like a South American polo player. But it just never felt right. Now, thinking about Will, my mouth can't help but curve into a dopey grin. "Will invented an organizational sleeve for his driver mirror to keep track of all his necessities" is all I say, and I don't need to say any more than that, because a best friend understands you to your core.

"Oh, no, he didn't." Ava humors me. "He's like your perfect, OCD Prince Charming. Sounds like he was made for you."

"And he smells so good," I say. "And his car . . . It's so clean."

"Stop, please, or I'll have to fight you for him," Ava says blandly, fanning herself with bored eyes.

"Shut up," I say, chuckling. "When he dropped me off it started pouring rain and, Ava . . ." I say, placing a hand on the shelf and turning toward her, to make sure she gets it: the importance of what I am about to say. "He came around to my side of the car to walk me to the door."

Ava starts walking back to the register. "When did it rain?" she wonders out loud.

I pause. "It *was* really odd. The whole thing was odd, actually. Will just appears all perfect out of nowhere, dying to go out with me, especially after what Lucy said."

"Lucy who?" Ava asks, sitting on the counter, and when I

explain about the author showing up in class, she looks at me as though I just ran over her cat. "Lucy Keating was at school today, and you did not tell me?"

"I'm sorry!" I say. "She's an old friend of Epstein's apparently." I shrug. "But honestly, you may wanna rethink your fandom. She completely freaked me out."

"What do you mean?" Ava asks.

"I don't even know how to say this out loud without sounding nuts. . . ." I start.

"I already think you're nuts," Ava deadpans.

"Fine." I shake my head. "She claimed to be writing my life."

Ava makes a face. "What?"

"Now you know how I felt!" I say, coming toward her and resting my hands on the counter next to her. "I don't even know a better way to explain it. All I know is Maya asked her what project she is working on, and she talked about a protagonist with my life. Grows up in Venice, happy, parents selling her childhood home, separating, even a weird little dog."

"That could be a lot of people," Ava says. "It doesn't mean she's writing about you."

"Except then I asked her about it, and she said she *was*," I say, and Ava's eyes go wide.

"What do you mean she said she was? Like, she's been stalking you?"

"No, that would almost be better than what she said! She said I am a character in her book. She said we all are." I make a "spooky" motion with my hands, as I walk back over to the bookshelves. This conversation is making me feel antsy.

"Oh, okay, so she's crazy," Ava states, raising her hands in the air. "Great. Just my childhood idol, a lunatic—toss that in the trash. No big deal."

I scrub at a spot on the bookshelf with the sleeve of my T-shirt distractedly.

"Wait, you don't actually believe her, do you?" Ava laughs.

I roll my eyes. "No," I say. "It's just been a weird day. I woke up, found out my parents were getting divorced, and then the most perfect boyfriend imaginable appeared out of thin air."

"I know it has." Ava grabs her coat and bag, and the big set of keys to the shop. "But even if we were both totally crazy, and actually believed Lucy, you still couldn't be a character in one of her books, because you aren't in a love triangle."

"What does that have to do with anything?" I ask.

"Love triangles are a Lucy Keating staple! She's never written a book without one," Ava says authoritatively, holding the door to the shop open wide. "Now let's go home before another perfect guy shows up and asks you to marry him this time."

6

Nope

WHEN AVA drops me off in front of my house that night, I hear the unmistakable sound of boys being stupid coming from the kitchen. I walk in to find Sam headbanging along with air guitar fingers as a pot of water boils over on the stove, and Elliot drumming on a few pots with wooden spoons. He stops when he sees me and slowly lays the spoons down, watching me, his expression unreadable.

"Your water is boiling," I say as I head to the fridge to grab a glass of water. Out of the corner of my eye I see Elliot reach over with one hand and turn down the burner. Then he speaks, but not to me.

"Your sister accepted a ride from a stranger this afternoon," he says to Sam, his eyes still on me.

"Yeah?" Sam has stopped headbanging, and is opening a box of pasta to pour it in the pot. "Who?"

"Yeah," Elliot says, hoisting himself up on the counter behind him with one swift movement and continuing to drum on his thighs. "Who?"

I take a cool sip of water from the glass. "Not that it's either of your business, but his name is Will Hale, and he just moved here from Hawaii," I say.

"Hawaii?" Sam says as though he's interested. But then he just says, "Sounds *lame*." He and Elliot burst into laughter and high-five.

"For your information," I tell them, "he's not lame at all. He's great. And he surfs, too. Without getting sand all over his car." The instant this last statement comes out of my mouth, I regret it. First of all, it's a stupid statement, and second of all, I'm digging into Elliot harder than usual, but I'm sick of his crap. My cheeks burn as I take another sip of water. Elliot is stirring a pot of tomatoes, but I can see the slightest twist of a smile on his face as he studies the pan.

"Okay," Sam says in his way that means *Who cares?*, "maybe we can take him out some time, show him the way it works in Venice. I gotta wiz." He walks down the hall, and I can't place it, but I am suddenly feeling awkward in this kitchen with Elliot. Elliot, who saw me projectile vomit at Disneyland when we were ten. Elliot, who knew when I got my period for the first time. I study his back, his loosely muscled shoulders, the place where his T-shirt stops and the smooth skin of his neck begins.

"Hey," Elliot says then, turning around quickly, deliberately, and I feel caught, like I have to explain myself.

"What?" I say defensively.

In response, Elliot's eyes widen. "What nothing," he says. "I was just gonna mention, if you will calm down for three seconds, that Paper Girl is playing at The Wiltern tomorrow night. I'm not going—we have band practice—but I thought I'd let you know."

I roll my eyes. "Thank you for the enthusiastic invitation," I say, "but I'm already going anyway."

Elliot blinks at me, and he turns back around to the stove. "Anytime," he says.

I take a few minutes to walk to the sink, place my glass in it, and head upstairs. I realize I'm waiting for him to ask who I'm going with, but he doesn't, and for some reason this only infuriates me more.

I'm sitting at my desk in Fiction class, considering the two major problems complicating my academic performance. Problems that, for once, I have no idea how to solve.

The first is that, despite all attempts, I am still useless at creative writing, and I am about to turn in yet another assignment that I hate. Epstein asked us to take a group of objects in our house and use them to tell a story. We could pick anything. I chose the contents of the produce drawer in our refrigerator, which seemed unexpected. But as I stared at the single tomato, bag of kale, and six clementines set in front of me on the kitchen island, all I could come up with was a story about shopping for groceries, where absolutely nothing interesting happened.

The second unfortunate issue is that directly to my right, gazing at me unapologetically out of the corner of his left eye, is Will. This doesn't sound like a problem, true, but it is when class participation may be all one has to get a decent grade, and one can't participate if one can't pay attention, and one can't pay attention with someone as cute as Will staring at them all the time.

"You're a published author, too, aren't you, Miss Epstein?" Maya asks. "Can't you tell us about *your* process?" I turn my attention back to the front of the class, where everyone is scrambling to ask more questions about what it's like to write a book, having been so inspired by Lucy Keating's talk yesterday.

Epstein flushes, a hand coming up to her cheek. She wears stacks of bracelets up each arm, and I've never seen her without them. They click and clack with her every movement.

"I do write my own series, but they aren't exactly appropriate for this age group." She hesitates.

"Why not?" someone asks, but I'm too busy catching Will's eye again to focus on who.

"I honestly shouldn't say." Epstein sighs. "I publish under a pseudonym. Let's just leave it at that. But I suppose I can talk to you a bit about how I work, if you'd like that?"

What Epstein doesn't realize is we all already know. We've always known. The whole school does. She writes bodice-ripper romance novels under a fake name, but nobody has ever been able to figure out which one. A group of freshman boys devoted their entire spring semester to it last year. But to our great surprise, Epstein covers her tracks well.

Will passes me a pen, which is confusing at first, since I didn't ask for one, until I see a thin piece of paper rolled around it like a scroll. It reads:

THIS IS A PUBLIC SERVICE ANNOUNCEMENT. IF YOU COULD REFRAIN FROM LOOKING SO GOOD IN ALL CLASSES SHARED WITH WILL HALE, IT WOULD BE APPRECIATED. HE IS TRYING TO GRADUATE. —SIGNED, THE OFFICE OF THE WELL-BEING OF WILL HALE

I set the note down, a tingling feeling bubbling up through my chest and spreading out through my shoulders and neck. It's awesome and horrible at the same time.

Without hesitating I turn the note over, and write a message back, sucking in my cheeks to keep from grinning.

Annabelle Burns will attempt to comply with the advisement as long as Will Hale ceases to stare at her with his irresistible grin. Do you agree?
—The Office of the Sanity of Annabelle Burns

I wrap the note and, using all my willpower, hand it back to him without meeting his eyes.

Less than a minute later the pen lands on my desk again, and when I open it, I have to fight my limbs from doing a happy dance. All it says is this:

NoPE.

"So, let's see," Epstein is saying. I have completely lost track of the conversation. We could suddenly be having this class at an aquarium, and I wouldn't have noticed. "Once I stumble upon the right idea, I'll write up a short pitch, work on some character development, and create an outline. I'll work off that until I have a manuscript, and after a few revisions I'll send it to my publisher."

"And then what happens?" Maya asks. She must really want to be a writer. It's cool she's taking it so seriously.

Epstein thinks. "Well, I've got my Editor, with a capital E, who works with me on the big picture. She helps shape the book into what it will be. Then I've got a copy editor, who goes through when the book is finished to query anything that doesn't make sense."

At this point, Margot Dunravey's hand shoots up in the first row. As far as I'm concerned, Margot and Napoleon belong in the same circle of hell. Margot and I have a few things in common: We're both driven, both straight-A students, both occasionally misunderstood. Here are a few things Napoleon and Margot have in common: They are both territorial, cutthroat, and have been known to growl when particularly frustrated.

My least favorite thing about Margot is that she always asks questions that everyone already knows the answers to. She doesn't even care what the answer is; she just wants the credit for asking. I ask a lot of questions, too, but at least mine are useful. Most of the time.

"You mentioned a copy editor points out things that don't make sense. What do you mean by that?"

"That's a good question Margot," Epstein says, barely hiding her surprise. "The Editor mostly focuses on the bigger picture, and making the story the best it can be. The copy editor catches any last issues, spelling mistakes, if it was four P.M. in chapter twelve, and in chapter thirteen it's suddenly nine A.M. two days earlier. My favorite example I always like to use is, my copy editor makes sure my characters don't have blue eyes in one scene, and brown eyes in another."

Margot nods and scribbles violently in her notebook, and my own hand shoots up.

"But why would they?" I ask in confusion.

"Why would they what?" Epstein asks.

"Why would they be blue in one chapter and brown in another?" I ask. "You're the author; you're writing it. Wouldn't you just know?"

Epstein lets out a tired breath. "Sometimes you forget. A book has a lot of words in it. You can get caught up in other things in the story, and it slips your mind. Don't you ever forget anything, Annabelle?"

"Not really," I say honestly. The whole classroom around me laughs.

"Well, lucky you." Epstein smiles, and leans back on her desk with her arms crossed. "Sounds like you've got copy editor potential. If anyone needs their stories proofread, Annabelle's your girl."

Just then another pen lands on my desk. When I unroll the paper this time, it says:

PICK YOU UP AT EIGHT?

I steal a glance at Will. He's pretending to listen to Epstein, leaning forward over his desk with his head resting between two fingers as he looks at her, but the smile on his lips is definitely for me. *The concert.* Out of nowhere I feel nauseous, but in a weirdly enjoyable way.

As class lets out, I hand the pen back to Will again. Written on the paper are two words:

Can't wait.

7

We Had a Slight Accident

"HOW ARE you doing, kiddo?" my dad asks when he walks into the kitchen that night, pulling a wool sweater over his head. I'm scrambling to finish up a problem set before Will gets here. I had trouble figuring out what color to put the concert under in my calendar. Was it really "Friends/Fun"? In the end, I decided to create a new color. A deep mauvy red. I labeled it "Romance." And then immediately wanted to hide from myself.

I look up and notice that The Evil One has trailed my father into the kitchen and is staring at me disdainfully. With my eyes, I dare him to snarl or bark, but I know he won't. Never in front of my dad. It's how Napoleon maintains his innocence.

Now I sigh and look my father in the eye. "I don't know how I'm doing," I answer honestly. I decided to shut that part of my brain off temporarily. If all else fails, that's what I do with the unknown. Ignore it until I can do something about it.

"Look, *you*," Dad says, and rests a hand on my shoulder. Napoleon twitches, but doesn't move. "You're a planner. You like to know what's coming. And I'm sorry we are putting you in a position where you don't have that security. But you have to trust Mom and me to make the right decisions here, and you have to focus on you. Finishing out the school year. What you're going to do this summer. Columbia. Let us handle the rest. Okay?"

I nod. "Okay," I agree.

"We love you. You and your brother. No matter how much things change around here, that never will. I'm not going anywhere," he says. "And neither is your mother."

This one I can't respond to. If I do, I might start crying, and I don't want to be blubbering when Will shows up. So I just nod.

"You wanna come for a walk with me and Napoleon?" he asks.

I snort. "No thanks."

"I thought not." My dad sighs. He looks down at Napoleon, who looks back up at him, waiting. "Come on, General," I hear him say as they walk off together toward the mudroom, Napoleon hustling happily at his side.

A few minutes later there is a light knock at the kitchen door, and Will is there, grinning with his hands in his pockets. He has on a gray T-shirt and worn-in jeans, and his cheeks are kind of flushed. He radiates warmth. "Hey," he says.

"Hi." I grin back. "You could've just texted from the car when you got here, you know."

Wills expression turns quizzical. "On a *date*? No way."

I grab my bag and pick up the jacket he lent me in the rain from a chair at the kitchen table. *You are going on a date*, I say to myself.

"Here," I tell him, holding out the jacket. "Didn't want to forget to give this back to you."

Will looks at the jacket and makes a face, his shoulders shrugging. "Nah, you keep that," he says. "I have an extra sweater for you in the car anyway."

It takes us thirty-five minutes to get to The Wiltern theater, and the scene outside is buzzing. It's in an iconic building in central LA, with a giant, split-level foyer in the shape of a circle.

"I like this place because it manages to fit a lot of people, but you almost never feel too far away from the stage," I tell Will over my shoulder.

"I can't wait." He smiles, and I feel his hand press gently against the small of my back as we make our way through the crowd. I shiver.

We find a spot down front, wedged into the corner of the venue. Paper Girl have just come onstage and the crowd is cheering like mad. They burst right into their big single, "Tell Me You Love Me," and people start to shimmy and move. The energy is electric. You can feel the love in this room.

Concerts always make me feel awkward and out of place, at least at first. Where to put my hands, how much talking is acceptable. I wish someone would just tell me how to move. But I go anyway, because I love the music, and I want to champion the situation. I want to be able to do it right. There's a girl in front of me, on the left, and she looks like she knows what she's doing. I keep one eye trained on her and follow her movements. When I glance at Will, he is grinning, slowly nodding to the music. He doesn't know what he's doing, either, I realize, which sets me at ease.

That's when I see Elliot a little farther down front, hopping from foot to foot as he bobs his head and moves his shoulders. Dancing was made for someone like him, with energy coming out the tips of his fingers. I stop still, suddenly on edge. Didn't he say he had band practice? Then he turns and looks directly at me. I watch his eyes find Will behind me, and he nods in greeting. We both wave back. Elliot hesitates, as though not sure if he should come over or not, but then he does.

"I thought you weren't coming," I say before I can stop myself, and Elliot pulls his head back.

"Well, here I am," he says.

I roll my eyes in response.

"Elliot, right?" Will yells over the music. "Good to see you, man." I shoot Will a look, but he doesn't notice.

Elliot casts a glance at me, and I force a stiff smile. They slap hands hello and are immediately engrossed in yelling over the music about how awesome the band is, because it's actually comprised entirely of influential members of other great bands. I chew the inside of my cheek. I don't want to seem difficult, but this just feels like all kinds of weird.

Two songs later Will goes off to see if he can scrounge up some beers, and Paper Girl slows it down, slipping into a song I love, that I was hoping they'd play: "She's the One." Before I can stop myself, a high whoop escapes my lips, and several people in my vicinity turn to stare. But most of them aren't judging; they're smiling. We're all fans. I turn to Elliot, an embarrassed hand over my mouth, my eyes wide, and he is chuckling, his whole face lit up. It makes me laugh, too.

I face the stage again and let the music sink in. I close my eyes and sway, and that's when I feel Elliot right behind me. Like, *right* behind me. My back is almost leaning into his chest, and I can feel his warmth on my skin. The music is liquid, pooling around us. He doesn't smell like Will, like cedar and detergent. He smells like deodorant and an unwashed T-shirt. He smells like boy. He smells like Elliot.

And the weirdest thought occurs to me. He smells . . . *good.*

And then in an instant Elliot is laid out flat on the ground, and his hand is holding his skull. A drumstick is on the ground by his side, and the singer is yelling, "Sorry, bro!" into the microphone, before the band picks up the tempo again. And as quickly as it all started, it's over, and I throw one of Elliot's arms around my shoulders and haul him out of the room.

"I can't believe I got hit by a drumstick," Elliot won't stop saying, his voice grainy and tired, as I move my finger in front of his nose. I am trained for this. I took an EMT class last year. "When has that ever happened? Barry Gross is one of the best drummers of our generation. I worship that guy! He is my idol. My idol just hit me with a freaking drumstick!"

"Shut up," I say. "What's your full name?"

Elliot frowns, but obliges. "Elliot James Apfel," he says.

"How old are you?"

"I am eighteen years old."

"What street do you live on?"

"Oakwood Avenue."

I roll my eyes. "That's where I live."

"Same thing," Elliot grumbles.

"What street do you live on, Elliot?" I ask again.

"Fourth Avenue." He sighs.

"What's the name of your band?" I ask.

"Don't have one." He smiles. "Remember?"

"You're a pain in the butt," I say, tilting my head.

"I know." He grins, and it all comes back to me for a second as I look down at him. That weird moment earlier, when everything felt like it was moving in slow motion. That moment

I found myself standing close to Elliot, breathing him in—and liking it.

"What happened?" Elliot and I both turn to see Will pushing his way out of the theater. "I got your text. Did you really get hit with a drumstick? Someone was talking about it at the bar."

Elliot just grumbles in response.

"We had a slight accident," I explain.

"Annabelle," Elliot interrupts. He looks so defeated, crouched against the building like that. "I wanna go home. I need Advil."

"Right," I say, thinking. "The only problem is, you really shouldn't drive right now, and I can't drive stick."

"Whatever," Elliot says. "I'll get Sam to drive me back tomorrow and pick up the car. Good advertising for the shop."

"Tomorrow it might be towed." I bite my lip.

"You worry too much," Elliot tells me.

"You don't worry *enough*," I push back, and it comes out flirtier than I intend it to. Or did I? Suddenly, my stomach is fluttering in a way I don't understand, and before I can figure out what any of it means, Will is offering to drive Elliot home. As he helps him off toward the car, I can't help feeling like somehow, I ended up on a date with both of them.

"I look like such an asshole," Elliot says from his position on the couch, legs propped up, a bag of peas resting atop his head.

"Good thing nobody cares," I shoot back, coming out of the

kitchen. I don't know what I was thinking before, back at The Wiltern, but I'm trying to forget about it as quickly as possible. "I made you some coffee. You shouldn't fall asleep for a few hours."

"Did you use the good beans?" Elliot asks petulantly.

"I know the way you like it," I reply, and I can feel Will watching me from his seat next to the TV.

"I should probably get going," Will says eventually. "Annabelle, can I drive you home?"

I spill the coffee a little bit as I set it down, unsure of how to answer. I know what the correct answer is. It's yes. Yes, you can drive me home because it's 10:15 and it's a school night, and also you're a total babe who smells like magic and packed an extra sweater for me without even asking. And you also didn't ask, "Do you need a ride home?" You asked, "Can I drive you?" because you are deliberate and you know what you want.

The weird thing is, a part of me wants to say no. A part of me wants to stay here on the couch with Elliot, doing nothing at all, making sure he doesn't fall asleep.

But that's crazy. I can't do that, for a million reasons. Because of the message it will send to Will, and because it's Elliot Apfel.

And then Elliot answers for me. "You should go, AB," he says. His brown eyes are surprisingly steady beneath the bag of peas, his voice level.

"But what about your head?" I ask. "What if you fall asleep and die?"

"My dad is here going through invoices in the garage. He'll

keep an eye out. And plus, there's a new episode of *Game of Thrones* I still haven't seen. I'll be okay."

I bite my lip. I look at Will, who is checking something on his phone.

"Really," Elliot says. "Go."

For some reason, this hurts. It surprises me, a tiny pain throbbing just below my rib cage. It makes me swallow. It makes me unable to meet his eyes. Would it kill him to be the tiniest bit grateful? Maybe a simple thank-you for saving him and, I don't know, an apology for ruining my date?

Or, it occurs to me, that maybe I just want him to want me to stay.

"'Kay," is all I manage to say. "Feel better." I grab my bag and walk out, and I don't stop moving until I'm in the passenger seat of Will's car. The magic cedar smell soothes me a bit, and when Will hops in next to me pulling a wool sweater over his head, a goofy grin on his face, the rest of the pain disappears.

"Okay, I have two options," Will says simply. "One: I could drive you home, which let's face it, is a pretty sorry end to a Thursday night."

"Uh-huh?" I ask suspiciously.

"Or two: You could tell me where a guy can find a decent ice cream cone in this town. Because I've been looking for days, and everything seems to be vegan, and I don't even know how a person makes vegan ice cream."

At this I can't help but put my hands over my mouth to hide my grin.

"What?" Will asks. "What's so funny?"

"You've come to the right place," I say in a tone that's all business. In my family, we say a pint of ice cream doesn't survive the night. I love it more than coffee. More than the newspaper. Maybe even more than running.

"Thank God," Will says dramatically. "Save me, Annabelle!"

"Head straight on Fourth, and take a right on Rose," I say. *And leave Elliot far behind.*

And just like that, we're off to finish the date we started.

Apparently, Sea Salt Creamery has a patio now, lined with extra-sparkly twinkle lights. They didn't last week, when I came with my dad. Now, here with Will, the effect is surprisingly romantic.

"When did you get these?" I ask the waitress who drops off our sundaes.

"I don't know." She shrugs, hardly looking at me. She reaches a hand behind her head to tighten her ponytail. "I know you said two scoops, but I gave you three." She tilts her head and smiles at Will.

I practically roll my eyes. Will might actually be perfect if he hadn't ordered a banana split. I've long had a squishy-fruit aversion.

"Everyone likes you," I say as the waitress walks off. The waitress, the people behind and in front of us in line, even this young couple's baby who wouldn't stop crying, but turned totally Gerber when Will leaned over its stroller. "Everywhere you go, people, like, swoon."

"That's not true," Will protests. "And besides, everyone likes you, too."

"No, they don't." I shake my head. "I mean, people don't hate me or anything; I'm nice, but they misunderstand me sometimes. Or I misunderstand them."

I bite my lip, and think about last week when Lee was showing off a new leather jacket she got for her birthday from Barney's, and I told her I'd seen one exactly like it on the Boardwalk for forty bucks. Ava told me the point was to compliment Lee's jacket. The point was not that she could have bought a cheaper one.

"I like that you're honest," Will says. "I'm this nice because my parents taught me it's how you have to be. But it means it's hard to know how they actually feel about anything."

"Well, maybe I can teach you to be more of a jerk." I smile.

"And I can teach you to be a pushover." Will grins. We meet each other's eyes a moment, and I relish in the fact that I am on a real date with a real guy, and I don't seem to have done anything awkward to mess it up yet.

"So, I wanna talk more about Annabelle Burns, the journalist," Will says.

I give him a look over my cone. "You *do*?" Other than my parents, I've never had someone be so interested in me before.

"I do." Will nods.

"What do you wanna know?" I ask.

Will looks off to the side for a moment, thinking. "So you like stories, as long as they're real?"

I shrug. "Yeah, that's one way of putting it. And I love to write. And edit. I love to take a group of words that just aren't working in harmony and turn them into something readable and interesting. I'm not sure there is anything more satisfying in the whole world."

"I've never thought about words like that before." Will chews on his spoon for a moment. "But you don't like fiction?"

I sigh. "It's not that I don't like it; I'm just not any good at it. And when it comes to reading, I prefer things that are actually real. Not made from someone's imagination. Why are *you* taking Fiction, by the way?"

Will scrunches up his nose for a second. "I guess I just thought it would be an easy class to come into at the last minute, after I transferred. But also, I thought it would be a fun challenge before I go off to college. See if I can really hack it." He grins widely, exuding optimism from the tips of his toes to the top of his head. "But back to more important matters," Will changes the subject. "You gotta have a bite." He scoops up a giant spoonful of his banana split, and holds it out to me.

"No thanks," I say. "I'm not a fan of bananas."

"Well, that's good," Will replies, "since this is a peanut-butter sundae." He gives me a weird look, and when I glance down, I am looking at a spoon with chocolate ice cream and a Reese's Peanut Butter Cup wedged into it.

Now, this is genuinely weird. I was there. I heard him order it. I thought to myself, *Yuck, bananas.*

Will is still waiting, and so is the spoon. "Quick, before it turns into a milk shake." His words are insistent but his tone is patient as ever. But my heart is beating a little bit faster.

"What's wrong?" Will asks. I close my eyes for a second. My skin is prickling.

I look up into Will's eyes to try to explain, but something is different here, too. His hair? His face? I can't figure it out, but perfect blue-eyed Will is just . . . not himself.

And that's when I realize he's actually not. Perfect blue-eyed Will's eyes are not blue right now. They're brown like Elliot's.

My copy editor makes sure my characters don't have blue eyes in one scene, and brown eyes in another, I hear Epstein say.

If anyone needs any of their stories proofread, Annabelle's your girl, I hear her say again.

"What's wrong with your eyes?" I ask Will.

"What do you mean?" Will replies, and blinks. And when he opens them again they are blue as ever.

He's too good to be true, I hear Ava say. *Sounds like he was made for you.*

"Annabelle?" Will asks, leaning closer. "Are you okay?"

And then the craziest thought occurs to me. What if Will *was* made for me? Or not made, but . . . written?

8

TK's Steakhouse

I MUST'VE banged on the door of Rosewater Café & Bookstore sixty times, and am seriously considering breaking in, when Ava suddenly appears behind the glass, looking like she's seen a ghost.

"Where were you?" I ask, my voice bordering on accusatory as I push past her, forcing her to take a few steps back.

"I was in the basement restocking," she says slowly, as though she's talking to the guy on the Boardwalk who sells portraits of John Travolta and only John Travolta. John Travolta as a deep-sea fisherman. John Travolta as Jesus. You get the idea. "We close at ten. What's wrong? Take a breath."

I take several breaths, placing my hands on my hips, before waving the syllabus for Epstein's class in her face. I ran all the way here, and now I'm out of breath. "I think she may have been telling the truth," I say.

Ava squints. "You're gonna have to give me a little more than that."

I sigh. "Will. He's so perfect, and he's so organized, and we're so similar, and he's so into to me . . ."

"You know that's not wildly shocking, right? That he's into you. You're smart and beautiful and sure maybe you have the personal interests of a senior citizen, which is a little weird, but—"

"That's not it! Listen." I run a hand through my hair. "Something has been off lately. Ever since Will got here. Sure, everything we have in common could be coincidence or fate or whatever, and his interest in me could be real, but then there's Lucy Keating and what she said, and then there was the ice cream and the eyeballs—"

"Still talking crazy," Ava cautions me. "Back it up." She sits on the counter, her legs dangling off. And I start from the beginning.

When I finish telling her about what happened at the ice cream shop, Ava thinks. "Are you sure you weren't just distracted? You know, by all his smoking hotness?"

I raise my hands in the air. "But it *was* a banana split!" I exclaim.

"You hate bananas," Ava states. Like she is president of the

Preservation of Annabelle Burns Society. I wait for her to say something else. To make sense of it all. To tell me everything is going to be okay.

Instead, she nods carefully. "Weird."

"Weird," I say.

"Did Will notice the changes?" she asks.

"Not only did he not notice the changes, it was like he rebooted himself," I say. "Like he'd been programmed. And . . . there's one more thing."

"What?"

"I think Elliot and I had a . . . I don't know. A thing? A moment? It's hard to explain. There was something there tonight, between us," I say.

"*What?*" Ava shrieks, and she looks like she's about to laugh. But she sees my face and stops. "No seriously. *What?*"

And then it all just comes out in a rush. I tell her about how he and Clara broke up, how he's been giving me this attention, and how he just showed up at the show tonight when he wasn't even supposed to be there. How funny that made me feel. How there was the energy, and then he got knocked out, and no sooner had that happened than Will showed up to save the day. When I finish Ava is just looking at me.

"But you hate Elliot Apfel," Ava says. "Just like you hate bananas."

"I *know*," I say, and fidget with a bracelet around my left wrist. "Ava, what if she was right?"

"Who?" Ava looks at me hard. "You cannot possibly mean Lucy Keating."

"But think about it. Will shows up, and he's perfect. But every moment he's not perfect . . . like when he offers me the wrong ice cream . . . he changes. Epstein told us all about copy editors fixing inconsistencies. Maybe that's what I saw in Will's eyes. Maybe Lucy forgot she made his eyes blue." I realize this sounds insane. But . . . what if?

Ava thinks for a moment. "Will does appear to be sent from heaven. I mean, if you asked my dad if you were a character in a book, he'd probably tell you anything is possible. He's also usually high, but it's food for thought."

Ava's dad was a rock star in the 1990s, and now he runs a retreat center in Malibu. He lets Ava throw all her birthday parties there. We take over the whole camp and roast marshmallows and roll out our sleeping bags in the community center, under a big Buddhist statue.

"But I mean, it's *not* true, right?" I say. "Because that would be crazy. I am not actually the main character in a book written by Lucy Keating."

Ava shakes her head. "It's not true, but I'll indulge you. You fire up the coffeemaker in the café. I'm going to find every Lucy Keating book we have, and we are going to look at the facts. Your favorite. Except that this time, the facts are fiction. Let's put those journalism skills of yours to good use."

Two hours and one giant pot of coffee later, I am standing in front of the chalkboard on which they usually write the specials. We've wiped it all off and at the top is written:

IS ANNABELLE IN A BOOK?

Below it the board is divided into two sections:

YES / NO

Ava leans back in a chair, her hands propped behind her head.

"Okay, in the Yes section: Annabelle Burns. Relatively adorable family unit with only minor, good-natured dysfunction. Perfect childhood home she is irrationally attached to."

I cringe. "Not for long."

Annabelle holds up a finger. "Major life disruption that includes possible divorce of loving parents, and the parents selling of the perfect childhood home, yet another signature Lucy Keating move. Sorry." She pauses and gives me an apologetic look.

Under YES I write: *family, house, divorce.*

"Lack of self awareness that she is strikingly beautiful."

"Oh, please," I say.

"Exactly," Ava says, and continues. "Utterly incredible dream boy that notices her in typical, classroom walk-in scenario."

"That did feel contrived," I mutter as I scrawl *dreamboy.* "And don't forget the small things. Like, I love sneaking weird snacks in the middle of the night, like the girl in *Something True*; I have a scar I got when I was little like the girl in *Across the Sea*; and I always have those nightmares about getting the wrinkles out of my bedsheets, like in *The Waking Hours*."

"Fine, but a lot of people have those things," Ava says. "Which is kind of the point. Accessibility, like Epstein told you in class. And here's what you don't have. You don't have any real hardship. Nobody is dying, for example."

"That's true, thank God," I say. "But Lucy specifically said in class that she is looking to give her characters Happy Endings right now."

"Right," Ava says. "But you still don't have a real love triangle. Because yes, Will is sent from heaven, but I don't care what you say—Elliot is an idiot. And he is not your guy."

"You're right." I nod. And she is. Elliot is the guy who moons people through windows while they're taking a test. He's carved his name into every desk he sits at. Last year he took over the school loudspeaker and played the Kinks at full volume for ten solid minutes, and nobody could ever prove it was him. "Thanks for setting me straight."

"You know what I think?" Ava asks.

"No, but I'm sure you are about to tell me," I say.

"I think this is a big deal. This thing with Will. No matter how much you have your crap together, boys are the one area where you really don't know what you're doing. And you hate that."

"Are you suggesting I'm looking for a reason for things not to work with Will?" I ask.

Ava makes a face. "Maybe?" she asks, and when she sees the look of annoyance on my face, she rushes to finish. "But honestly, what I'm saying is I don't blame you! This stuff with your parents is really hard. And we're graduating soon. And, honestly, isn't everyone kind of having an existential crisis right now? All this stuff can be scary. So my advice? Take things slow with Will. Let him prove to you how real he is."

I bite my lip, and lay the piece of chalk down on the counter-top. "You're a really good friend, you know that?" I tell her.

Ava rolls her eyes. "Yes, I do."

It's not the brightest idea to walk home by myself at three A.M. in our neighborhood, but I know how to do it as safely as possible, and I need a little room to breathe. I stick to the big streets, meaning I take Venice Boulevard to Abbot Kinney, which was just named The Coolest Street in America to the great displeasure of all the long-time residents. "How many juice shops does one block really *need*?" my dad asked out loud a few months ago, and my mom told him he was acting like an old person.

"But isn't *old* cool?" he asked then, genuinely interested. "Dad bods and normcore? Isn't that what the kids are into?"

"And juice, apparently," she replied, and went back to reading her book, while my dad smiled at her.

It was these moments, I thought, that made them so good together. Now I find it confusing and sad to think about exactly how much was going on below the surface.

I keep making my way down The Coolest Street in America, and something odd happens. I pass TK's, my favorite restaurant since I was a kid, an old neighborhood steak joint where I celebrate every birthday. It has big red leather booths, and giant hot fudge sundaes. Then I stop, and back up a few feet, noticing for the first time that the shop sign next to TK's, a store I've never been to that specializes in European sneakers, says the same thing, but this time without the *s*: TK. And so does the sign after that, a floral shop, the two letters written in a loopy script.

I start walking again, slowly. What happened to all the shop signs? I wonder if someone is shooting a movie, which is often the case—last week they turned a boutique near our house into a coffee shop so they could shoot a TV show there—but I don't see any production trailers or lighting equipment. And more important, why does TK sound so familiar?

I Google *TK* on my phone as I walk, and directly under "TK's Steakhouse," there is a Wikipedia entry, and when I read it, my breath catches in my throat.

> **TK**—A publishing term meaning To Come.
> Used to signify where additional material will
> be added at a later date.

And now I remember where I heard TK used. In class yesterday while I was flirting with Will. Epstein said she uses it when she wants to come back and fill something in.

I look up again, scanning the length of Abbot Kinney. TK after TK, with the exception of one place: Electric Café, where we get The Good Coffees.

A place Lucy Keating would already have a name for, since she just wrote about it.

Without realizing it, I break into a run. My life is filled with TKs, because my life does not belong to me.

My life belongs to Lucy Keating.

9

The Egtved Girl

I WAKE up to the sounds of low snorts coming from behind my closet door, and throw it open to reveal Napoleon, burrowing into my laundry bin.

"*Out!*" I cry. Napoleon wiggles out butt first, looks at me indignantly, and maintains complete eye contact for the duration of his exit from the room.

My mother pokes her head in. "Everything okay in here?" she asks.

Well, let's see, I want to tell her. *My life is probably being written by a commercial romance author, making me question literally everything I do and say, not to mention my fundamental existence.*

I barely slept last night, not that there were a lot of hours left to sleep, and instead just lay in my bed staring at the ceiling going over every part of my life for which I had assumed I was responsible. Every part I thought belonged to me. Now I feel like I would need to run for thirty miles just to wind myself down. My world is off-kilter, and there is nothing I can do about it.

"I feel sick," I say instead, giving as honest an answer as possible.

My mom lays a cool hand against my forehead. "You don't feel warm," she says. "Do you want to tell me what's going on? Is this about me and Dad?"

"No," I say quickly.

"Because we haven't really gotten to talk about it more . . ." she starts to say. "You were out so late last night. . . ."

"It's not about . . . that." I can't even say the word *divorce*, so I begin making my bed. My mom joins me, pulling the sheet straight on the other side, not saying anything. Knowing I'll begin when I'm ready.

"I just feel like life suddenly got so out of control," I say honestly. "I keep thinking about why things happen, and what the meaning of it all is. Does any of it even matter?" I don't tell her about Lucy Keating. I'm pretty sure it is bizarrely, insanely real, but I can't even imagine saying it out loud to her yet.

"Honey, everyone feels that way at some point at your age. Probably many times, even during a lifetime. It's called growing."

She goes to grab a pillow that's fallen on the floor. "Your father and I never wanted to do the helicopter-parent thing. If we made all your decisions for you, you'd never know what you really wanted. You would never have wanted anything for yourself. And look at you!" She holds a hand out. "You got some of our best qualities, and plenty of great qualities we never came close to having. You've always known what you want, and you've always gone for it without even hesitating."

"But what if I don't know what I want anymore?" I ask.

"Then that's okay, of course," she says, looking at me as she sets the pillow on the bed. "You're seventeen, honey. You have your whole life to figure it out. What's the rush?"

I fold a throw blanket at the edge of my bed, and take a step back, deep in thought. I just can't seem to get it straight in my head. If everything I thought I wanted was an idea or decision designed by Lucy Keating, then what would I want if Lucy Keating wasn't deciding it for me?

"Does this have anything to do with Elliot?" my mom asks out of nowhere, and I jerk to attention. My mother knows everything. She knows when I'm upset before I even say so. She knows what outfit will look best on me when we go shopping, even if I originally snub my nose at it. But for once, she's wrong.

"There's nothing going on with Elliot," I blurt out, then realize that's not really what she asked, and my cheeks flush.

"You know he's always had a thing for you," she says.

"Mom!" I say. "This is zero of your business. Besides, Elliot and I can't stand each other."

My mother just smiles, walking out of the room. "If that's what you think, you have a lot to learn about men." She pauses in the doorway. "We don't have to talk about it now. Any of it," she says. "But whatever it is, I'm here if you need me. In the meantime, go to school. You know I'd let you stay if you wanted to, but we both know you'll be mad at yourself later if you don't go."

I sigh, knowing she's right. Again.

A couple of hours later, I'm speeding along the path at school, my destination in sight. There is only one truly gross, completely run-down building on the entirety of my high school campus, and oddly enough, it also happens to be my favorite place on Earth.

Cedar Spring was built on the bones of an old convent, which I originally thought would mean sparse décor and minimal light and lots of tiny, windowless rooms. Isn't that what nuns do all day? Pray in tiny rooms? But instead the school is comprised almost entirely of white clay structures topped with classic red tile roofing. And since a lot of celebrity kids go here, anything that wasn't already beautiful was made to be so.

Except the office of the *Cedar Spring Gazette*, which resides in a small, now-defunct utility building, all metal and exposed piping and Sheetrock. But it is also filled with light. Windows span from floor to ceiling, and there's even a giant skylight where the roof should be. I'm not sure why a skylight was ever necessary in the original design, but regardless I am grateful for it.

The desks in the office are a million years old, and the place hasn't been cleaned out since the club was founded. Chewing gum lines the bottom of every table, layers and layers of tape stick to the walls, not to mention there are so many pushpin holes you'd think the whole structure was about to cave in. The administration has offered to move us a bunch of times, but there is a certain pride in the place. It's where we suffer, where we toil late into the night, all for the greater good of our small, six-hundred-student population.

The *Gazette* is my place. It's where I can go to be alone between classes. And it's where I really shine. I put on some giant headphones and work off an old Apple computer in the corner and nobody bugs me until the afternoon, when the club meets to assign stories.

The thing is, I like to check things off. I like to put a bunch of stories on the board and then draw a nice pretty line through them once they're done. I like to fill in the slate every week. It's why I applied to Columbia, where I plan to major in journalism and intern at all the best news stations in New York. I know I'm not even a legal adult yet; I know my mom said there's a lot to figure out. But one thing I know about my future: Lucy Keating or no Lucy Keating, there will be words involved.

So if I can just get in there, just find someone who needs me to look at their latest piece of writing, or fix a layout issue with Hector, a budding graphic designer who I poached from the Art Club last semester, then I think I'll start to feel a little more like myself again. The me that existed before—

"Hey!" I hear from behind me, and cringe a little bit, before finally turning around and plastering a small smile to my face.

But the smile becomes real when I see Will standing there, with his gray Will-like chinos and his plaid, Will-like button-down shirt; his long, fluffy Will eyelashes batting; and his cute Will mouth in a small smirk.

I hate what I am about to do to him.

"How's your morning?" he asks good-naturedly. "Feeling better?"

I don't blame him for checking in after I completely wigged out at the ice cream shop last night. I managed to pull it together and stick out the rest of the date, but something was definitely off, and he noticed. Not to mention I practically ran out of his car before he could kiss me. Not that I didn't *want* to, exactly; I just had some other things on my mind. Like whether he was real or not.

"Feeling better," I answer. "Thanks for asking."

"What about a redo?" Will gazes down at me, and once again I get lost in his eyes. "You know, one that doesn't get interrupted by a head injury? I found this cool Vietnamese place around the corner from school. I thought we could go at lunch." Ray Woods, our social chair, captain of our basketball team, and Nisha's greatest obsession, walks by and they share a quick nod and a handshake. Then Will looks back at me. I choose not to comment on the fact that he has been here for merely a few days, and is already on bro terms with one of the most respected guys in our school.

"I can't, Will," I say, and start walking in the direction of the *Gazette* again.

"Why not?" he asks, all innocent and sweet, as he follows me down the path.

"I have somewhere I need to be," I say cryptically. *A hole to hide in*, I add to myself. Somewhere to get away from all this, and to maybe even figure out what the hell is really going on.

"I'll go with you," Will suggests matter-of-factly. Over on the right the girls' varsity tennis team is splayed out on the lawn, eyeing him like a pride of lionesses ready to pounce. He doesn't even notice.

"No," I finally turn and say directly. "You cannot come."

Will frowns, thinking, and I feel awful. He doesn't deserve this. But then again, he isn't even real. Thanks to Lucy Keating, he's like a romantic punching bag. Before he can respond, I do.

"It's nothing personal, Will. Really. Last night was fun. I'm just behind on a lot of stuff. I need to go handle some things. I'll see you later. Okay?" And before he can say another word, I lose myself in the sea of people heading to first period.

And yet, despite my best efforts, Will is everywhere I need to be today. I should be thrilled by this, the fact that I can't escape him. That he's in the *Gazette* room, being interviewed for an article about what it's like to be "new" only months before school is over.

That he's giving a presentation in my physics class, which he isn't even *in*, on a small solar-powered car he designed at his old school.

That at an all-school meeting, I get stopped on the way by Dr. Piper and the only seat left is next to him.

I should be thrilled by it all, and by how thrilled he is to see me, but I'm not. I can't think with him around. And right now, I really need to think.

At four P.M. I burst through the doors of the library, and find Nisha, Ava, and Lee draped over various chairs and tables, pretending to do their homework. They acknowledge me with bored nods, and I settle in peacefully, and open my computer to scan today's *New York Times* for interesting articles. Something pops up that says "More Facts Discovered about Teenager from the Bronze Age."

My interest piqued, I click the link, and end up reading an article about the Egtved Girl, who was dug up almost one hundred years ago, and is believed to date back thousands of years before that. Originally, scientists believed she was native to the town in Denmark where she was found, but further scientific analysis has discovered she may have traveled great distances, and seen a great deal of her region of the world.

"Probably because nobody was writing her story without her consent," I whisper to myself.

Two minutes later, the door to the library swings open again, and I don't even have to look up to know it's Will. It would be anyway, and also all my friends just got weird and fidgety.

"The Egtved Girl," Will says, peering over my shoulder, and the hairs on the back of my neck stand on end. "I read about her earlier today. So cool, right? She surprised us all."

Despite wanting to escape him, I soften at this thoughtful comment. "That's exactly what I was just thinking," I say, and Will smiles, pulling up a chair and sitting down next to me.

"Are you still busy?" he asks. I am about to tell him yes, but when I see the look of pure adoration in his eyes, what ends up coming out is "Not really."

"Good." He grins. "I got you something."

"Why?" I groan. Why does he have to be so perfect? But he doesn't seem to notice.

"It's called *The Elements of Style*." Will pulls a slim book out of his backpack. "We used it at my old school. I know you said you're having a hard time in Epstein's class, and this is, like, the go-to, old-school manifesto on the rules of writing. It doesn't discuss creative writing much, but I thought it might remind you why you fell in love with words in the first place. Structure, organization, simplicity."

I open the book and flip to a page:

> *"It is an old observation," he wrote, "that the best writers sometimes disregard the rules of rhetoric. When they do so, however, the reader will usually find in the sentence some compensating merit, attained at the cost of the violation. Unless he is certain of doing as well, he will probably do best to follow the rules."*

I look up. "Will," I say. "This is one of the nicest things any-one has ever given me."

Will just shrugs. "Do you really like it?"

"I love it," I tell him, and I mean it.

Will bites his bottom lip, and suddenly, I feel like we are the only two people in the room.

"Also, hey"—he clears his throat and turns to my friends—"I'm throwing a big party at my parents' place this weekend. I know it's kinda weird since I'm so new, and I'm still getting to know everyone. But it's their gift to me since they uprooted me from my old school with basically no notice."

"A party?" Nisha asks, her eyes are huge, and she looks like she might dance on top of the table, she's so excited. Ava's hands are clasped together like a Disney princess.

"A big one," Will says conspiratorially.

A whoop erupts from their chairs, causing a shush from the librarian, but I continue to sit there, thumbing through the pages of the book. It's filled with deliberate, beautiful language on what makes a good paragraph, and even a list of "words commonly misused." I'm sure most of my friends would fall asleep reading this, but to me it's perfect. And the fact that Will would know this bewilders me.

"Annabelle, you'll come, right?" I hear him ask imploringly.

My head feels like it's filled with fog. Should I go? This is insanity. He might not even be real. *I* might not even be real. But it's just a party.

I look up at my friends' eager faces, at Will's questioning eyes, and back down at the book in my hand. "I'll think about it."

10

Where Warmth Begins

WHEN MY dad picks me up from school that afternoon, he says we have to stop by the vet to pick up Napoleon.

"What did he do this time?" I ask.

"I don't like your tone," my father says, just as we're crossing Washington Boulevard. "But for your information, it seems his intention to eat all our socks and underwear has caused a bit of a blockage. He's going to be okay, but they had to sedate him."

"They always have to sedate him," I say. Napoleon has had three vets and six groomers since he's been a member of our family. When you call to make an appointment, they just say,

"Oh." Maybe that's one of the reasons he's so mean. Everyone keeps breaking up with him.

In the linoleum-floored waiting area, we sit in plastic-backed chairs, surrounded by unhappy felines and morose hounds. One chubby little terrier is pulled back into an exam room butt first, his front paws stretched out in front of him desperately, as though headed toward certain death. "It's just a checkup, Harvey!" his human companion exclaims.

My father reads a script on his iPad, and I open *The Elements of Style*, thinking about Will.

> **Part II, Article 17:** *A sentence should contain no unnecessary words, a paragraph no unnecessary sentences, for the same reason that a drawing should have no unnecessary lines and a machine no unnecessary parts. This requires not that the writer make all his sentences short, or that he avoid all detail and treat his subjects only in outline, but that he make every word tell.*

I sigh happily, but as the breath exits my body, a nervous feeling replaces it. The more I think about Will the swoonier I get, and the swoonier I get the more confused I become. I mean, could Will really be written for me? Am I really just a character Lucy Keating created? Is everyone? I glance over at my dad. And worse: Did Lucy Keating seriously construct my parents' divorce just to add a plot layer to my story? An "inciting incident," Epstein would call it. It frustrates me that in the back of my mind I can still hear Lucy's voice, telling me this was all her plan. What did I do to deserve this?

Feeling restless, I put down *The Elements of Style* and decide to Google Lucy Keating on my phone, where a new *Interview Magazine* article pops up. It's a photo of the author on a sunny chaise at an old-Hollywood type haunt, and the title reads: "The Irony and the Ecstasy: Lucy Keating was known for her tragic endings. Could the collapse of her marriage have finally turned her into a romantic?"

Q: You recently went through a fairly private divorce with a fairly high-profile man, Edwin Clarke, the youngest-ever CEO of Clarke Industries, which owns two of the biggest media agencies in the world.

LK: [Smiling] Is there a question in there?

Q: Forgive us. We're prying.

LK: Edwin and I met at Brown. We were English majors, aspiring writers. Everything was different then. I got an MFA; he got an MBA`.`.`. let's just say that sometimes people can change together, and sometimes they can't.

Q: Did the heartache over the breakup inform any of your work?

LK: Not yet. But oddly enough, I had found kind of a cult following in the tragic. People read my books knowing they would go from up to down again, that in the end they were going to get a good cry out of it.

Q: But not anymore?

LK: I've done enough crying.

Q: So where do you go from here?

LK: Well, a lot has changed for me in the past year or so. Now I'm in sunny California. I just adopted another dog. He's a pain in the butt, but I love him. I want to try and take myself a little less seriously. I want my characters to be happy.

Q: And how's that going?

LK: I'm getting some pushback.

Q: From your editors?

LK: [Smiling again] From my characters.

Well, this pisses me off. I mean, excuse me for having an opinion on my life being a total freaking construct. I realize how ridiculous I sound, and I want to scream, but then I glance up to notice the women next to me reading over my shoulder.

"Sorry." She gives a bashful shrug. "I just love her."

I attempt a smile.

"You know they're making *Across the Sea* into a movie?" the woman asks.

"I didn't," I answer, and in my head I wonder, *If my story became a movie, who would play me?* Then I shake the image from my mind. This is all bananas.

"Who are you waiting for?" I ask, nodding toward the exam rooms and trying to change the subject.

"Tuna," she answers.

"A fish?" I ask, surprised. I didn't realize people took their pet fish to the vet.

"Tunafish is a hamster," the woman clarifies then, and I can't seem to find the right words to respond to this.

The vet comes out through the swinging doors and walks over to her, holding a small shoe box. "He's still a little groggy, but he did very well," he says. Tunafish's human companion thanks the vet profusely and my father gives me a look over the top of his iPad, then notices the book in my lap.

"Where'd you get that?" my dad asks, pointing to *The Elements of Style* after Tuna and his caretaker have left.

"A friend," I say, feeling my cheeks get warmer.

"A boy?" my dad asks, with raised brows.

"Yeah, a boy," I answer.

"I remember that book from college. He must really like you," he observes.

"Why do you say that?" I ask, my voice getting weird and high.

"Because he must really be paying attention," my dad replies, looking back at his iPad with a small smile.

I'm in a weird mood when I open the door to my bedroom at home, which makes the sight of Elliot, lying on my couch and reading my creative-writing notebook, particularly infuriating.

"These stories suck," he tells me.

"I know," I say, snatching it out of his hand and walking over to my desk. "But thanks for your support. And also, get out of my room."

"I am being supportive, Bellybutton," Elliot explains, sitting up. "You're a quasi-genius. You win awards for your writing. And those stories look like they were written by, well . . . *me.*"

"Can you leave?" I ask again.

"Whoa," Elliot says, holding his hands high in the air like he's not responsible for whatever is happening on my face. "Annabelle. Relax. I'm kidding."

"No, you're not," I say, my voice starting to shake. "They suck, I know. I don't even want to be taking this stupid class. I have to. Do you think I like being bad at school? Failing doesn't come so easily to all of us." This last part was unnecessary, I know, but I need him out of here. His presence is a reminder of just how out of control my life is becoming.

"Is there a shot you can take when your bitchiness becomes

unchecked? Because if so I will gladly give it to you," Elliot retorts.

"Good one," I say.

"You asked for it," he says back.

"No, I didn't, actually," I say. "I didn't ask for you to be in here. Why are you always in here?!"

Elliot raises his hands silently again, his face still, and starts to walk toward the door.

"I don't even know how to explain it," I hear myself say, rearranging the top of my desk over and over again to try to calm myself down, before laying my head in my hands. My eyes have become wet. "Do you ever just feel like your life is, like"— how can I even explain this to him—"written for you?"

To my surprise, Elliot stops, and nods. "Sure," he says.

"Really?" I look up.

"Yeah, really."

"Then what do you do?"

"I give it the middle finger," Elliot says seriously, and a small laugh escapes my lips.

I think about how I tried to avoid Will all day, but he kept showing up, and then he gave me that freaking book, the sweetest thing imaginable. All I wanted was to get away from the person—the character—Lucy Keating had written for me, but then there he was, being so . . . great.

"But what if you can't? What if you try and it doesn't work?"

"Is this about your parents?" Elliot asks, sitting down on my bed. "Because I've been there."

"It's not about them!" I cry, and I want to throw something. But maybe it is, in a way. Maybe it's about the fact that a week ago my life was great. Maybe not perfect, but pretty close. I had it all under control. And now I don't know anything anymore. I don't even know what's real.

"Annabelle, if you don't like the way your life is going . . . rewrite it," Elliot says, having no idea how much sense he's making. He's leaning over and wresting his elbows on his thighs, the closest he's been to me since the concert.

"I'm trying," I whimper.

"So keep trying," he says back. "You worry too much."

"Okay," I say, taking a deep breath. He's still so close, and just then I have an insane urge to stick my head in the crook of his neck, and keep it there. Will may smell like laundry, but Elliot smells like warmth. He smells like where warmth begins.

"Annabelle?" Elliot asks.

"Yeah?" I say, and look up at him.

"You have mascara all over your face," he says instead. And instead of sticking my head in the crook of his neck, I smack him in the shoulder.

"*Ow*," he says loudly, but then he grins. "I should get downstairs. We got band practice. Clara or no Clara." He stands up and heads toward the door, and pauses, letting the top of his hand graze the top of the frame. "Hey, are you going to that guy Will's party this weekend?"

I snort. "I like how you say That Guy Will, like you didn't

just third-wheel it on our date the other night. You know, after I rescued you."

"Fine, *Will's* party. Are you going or not?" Elliot asks.

I straighten up a little bit, wiping at my eyes, wondering why he's asking. "Um," I start, "I think so."

Elliot crosses his arms over his chest for a second, thinking. I expect him to tell me he's got a gig or a photography exhibit or a skateboarding show. Elliot's scene is not high school. It's never really been high school.

"Me too," he says instead. "I'll see you there."

"You will?" I squeak.

"If you're going," he says, heading out the door now. Not flirtatiously. Not like the time he mentioned the sand on my jeans. Like he's stating a fact. Like he's telling me how he takes his coffee.

"Elliot!" Sam cries then, from outside the door. "Where are you, man? We gotta practice."

Elliot jerks to attention. "Gotta bounce," he says. "See you."

And just like that he's gone, out the door.

"Why are you always in there?" I hear Sam's muffled voice from the hallway as the sound of boy feet charging down the stairs dissipates.

"Why am I always where?" is the last thing I hear Elliot say, and the sound of his voice makes me smile.

11

You're a Killer Emotional Support Pony

"I THINK I'm in love," Ava says, her face upside down. She's lying on the beach blanket with her head next to my legs. To celebrate how long it's been staying light every day, we decided to pick up some poke from Papa's Poke Shop after school and head down to the water. The sky is glowing pink, which is perfect for our conversation.

"You're always in love," I reply, smiling as I manage to grab a chunk of deliciously seasoned tuna, a piece of avocado, and some brown rice all in the same bite. *Ice cream and poke*, I think. That's all I need to survive.

"This time I mean it," Ava says.

"You always mean it," I say. "Who is it this time?"

"Navid." She sighs.

"Good choice," I say, pleasure in my voice. Ava's past boyfriends include such stellar human beings as the angry, heavily tattooed singer of a local punk band, or an insecure member of the school's improv troupe. But Navid is a straight-A student, president of the senior class, and genuinely nice to everyone. Not to mention his eyes may be the very definition of smoldering.

"So what's the game plan?" I ask.

"He's going to be at Will's party," Ava says. "They bonded in AP Bio."

"That makes sense," I say. "They're both creepily perfect."

"They'll probably run for president someday on the same ticket," Ava says, and we both crack up. "Hey!" she says. "We could have side-by-side offices at the White House!"

I know Ava's joking, but my face falls anyway, because something about that feels wrong. I've already told Ava all about what happened when I left the bookstore the other night, about all the TK signs, basically proving that we are in fact living through one crazy, confusing YA story, starring *me*. Written by some loony tunes author who is actually bizarrely in her own story. And of course Ava believes me, because she's Ava. Because she's the best.

I can see Will in my head, picture exactly how right he is for me, but there's still something missing.

"What is it?" Ava asks.

"Nothing," I say. "It's complicated."

Ava thinks for a second. "Maybe you don't want to share the White House with me, because you don't want to share the spotlight," she says quietly, digging in some sand, and I almost drop my next bite of poke.

"What are you talking about?" I ask, placing my fork back in the bowl.

"Come on, AB," Ava says. "We all know what I am in this story. If you are the protagonist, and Will is your love interest, then what am I? I'm the best friend. And what do we know about the best friend?"

"What do we know?" I repeat.

"They're one-dimensional!" Ava cries, sitting up. "They exist purely to get the main character to talk about their actions, to figure out their problems. They cause the breakthroughs, but they usually have nothing to call their own." She starts to pack up her stuff in a huff.

"Wait, you're really upset about this?" I ask, and Ava just shrugs without looking at me. "Ava, I mean it, I don't want the spotlight. You know me. I'm the one who gets embarrassed when you guys are loud at lunch. I don't *want* any of this." My voice cracks. I never even considered how Ava might feel about all this, and it kills me that, after everything she does for me, I could ever make her feel like I don't appreciate how amazing she is. "Please, you're my best friend. I love you. You can't be mad at me."

Ava sighs, and drops her hands by her side. She sits back on her heels and gazes at the ocean. "I just don't want to be your emotional support pony," she admits.

I struggle to keep a straight face. "What is an emotional support pony, exactly?" I ask. In front of us, out on the water, a big sailboat passes directly into frame, its sail perfectly taut against the wind. I want to swim out to it and get as far away from here as possible.

Ava snorts. "I saw this thing on the nature channel about a horse farm in Virginia. Sometimes the new horses get really worked up and anxious, so they have these small, fuzzy, emotional support ponies that hang out with them in their pens. Apparently, it's soothing."

We stare at each other for a moment, and then start cracking up at the same time. "Fine. I guess I'm being ridiculous. But this whole thing is weird," Ava says.

"So help me figure out what's going on," I say. "You may be the only one who can."

Ava nods, thinking, then scooches off her knees, settling back down on the blanket. "I know I've already told you this, but I'm not sure this is something that can be figured out so easily. Love, relationships, this is the one area where we are not in control. Do you like Will or not?"

I pause. "I like Will a lot," I say.

"But you like Elliot, too?" she asks.

"I didn't say that," I reply.

"You didn't have to," she says. "I see him dropping you off almost every day. He's usually late. You are never late. And you let yourself be late . . . for Elliot."

"That's not about Elliot," I protest. "That's because stuff is weird with my parents. The more time I spend with them, the more I might have to talk about . . . you know."

"Well, maybe it would be a good idea for you to talk about You Know," Ava says.

I wave my hand dismissively. "No. And no to Elliot, too. I like Will," I say. "I really do. Will is charming and fun to look at, and he makes me feel like a spotlight is shining on me whenever we're together. Like I'm the most interesting person in the world, and so is he, but he finds me more interesting than him."

"That's a little hard to follow, but I think I get it." Ava nods.

"I don't have feelings for Elliot; we just know each other really well. He understands a part of me other people don't. He knows how to call me out."

"That's because there's real history there," Ava says.

"But that doesn't mean it's love," I say.

"And it doesn't have to be!" Ava cries, throwing her hands in the air. "That's what I'm trying to tell you. You have no idea where either of these relationships is headed. Do you remember Jake Schwartz?"

I lie back, covering my eyes with one hand. "How could I forget? He's the only guy who has ever dumped you, by my recollection."

"And I will forever loathe him for messing up my perfect record," Ava mutters. "But do you remember when I first met him at summer camp? He seemed perfect! It was a romance for the ages. And then I went to visit him in Cincinnati. Do you remember what happened? Do you remember the lizards?" She is leaning over me now, an intense look on her face.

"Yeah, that sucked. I'm sorry." I stare up at her, sliding my hand over my mouth to hide my smile.

"He had a bedroom *full* of lizards!" Ava exclaims, throwing her hands in the air. "Wall to wall! He had neglected to tell me, in all our deep, emotional connection"—she rolls her eyes—"that his true life passion was reptiles."

I nod my head, keeping my mouth tightly shut so I don't laugh. Because that would really set her off.

"My point is, if you'd asked me that summer what would happen with me and Jacob, I would've said he was the man of my dreams! We never fought once. We had everything in common. We were crazy about each other. But sometimes life has other plans. Sometimes people take time to reveal themselves to you. Who knows, you could go to Will's house tonight and he could have a bedroom *full* of lizards."

"I doubt it," I say.

"But you don't know," she says back, and I can't argue with that.

I stare at the horizon line for a moment. "The thing that's killing me is that sometimes I think I can feel her in my head.

I've begun to doubt my own thoughts, because I'm worried Lucy Keating is writing them."

"Okay, well, say this is true," Ava ponders aloud. "I get it; she's like God. But she's not everywhere. Where's the one place a writer never writes about? Where nothing interesting usually happens?" Ava breaks into a slow smile.

"I don't know," I say in bewilderment.

Ava is now in full-out grin mode. "The bathroom," she says.

"Gross!" I yell.

"Gross or not, it's your only way out. If you're feeling a little nuts, go sit in the bathroom until your head clears. Now, let's get out of here; we need to figure out what we're wearing to this party." She grabs her tote bag and the blanket and starts walking toward the Boardwalk.

"Hey, Ava?" I say as we walk back along the Boardwalk, passing tattoo parlors and vendors who are packing up their art for the day, and all the things that make this beach so crazy—like the guy who walks around in a *Star Wars* stormtrooper uniform. "You're so much more than a sidekick to me."

"I know," she says, turning around and wrapping an arm around my waist.

"But you are a killer emotional support pony," I say quietly, and she gives me a playful shove.

When I get home from the beach, Mathilda Forsythe is standing on my lawn, watching The House like she is waiting for it to answer a question. I look at her, and she looks back, providing no explanation.

"What are you doing here?" I ask.

Just then my mom walks outside, wearing worn-in jeans and a linen sweater. "Oh, honey, you're back earlier than I expected." She hesitates, but puts on a bright smile. "Mathilda is interested in buying The House."

I feel instantly nauseous. This is all wrong. This house can't belong to Mathilda, with her limited conversation and her black ensembles. This has to go to a family. With a brother and sister, and a small dog with an attitude problem. I think fast.

"Did you tell her that the heat only works half the time?" I say, placing my hands on my hips.

"Annabelle," my mother says. "Cut it out. Mathilda knows it all. She wrote about the place, after all." And to Mathilda, she says, "I'm sorry, Annabelle is having a hard time adjusting to the move."

"Does she know the upstairs toilet spins the wrong way?" I blurt out.

"That's not even true!" my mother exclaims.

"It could be." I jut my chin out. "Now you'll always wonder. Also, the neighbors always park in front of our garage, no matter how many times we tell them not to. And they throw tons of parties that go late into the night. Nobody gets any sleep around here."

"Well, now you are just making stuff up," my mom says, the color rising in her cheeks. "Go to your room."

"Not my room for *long*," I announce, and march into The House. I sit on my bed for a minute, my whole body vibrating. I should go for a run, even if it's about to get dark. I get up and start pulling on my gear.

This is all unfair, and it's happening too soon. They can't just tell me they're separating one week, and sell the whole house the next. Especially not to Mathilda. She doesn't belong here. I plug my headphones into my ears and jog downstairs, ready to burst through the front door, but decide to detour and give my parents one last piece of my mind.

"You know what?" I announce as I march through the doorway, and then stop. The living room and the kitchen are empty. There is nobody around to even be mad at.

Just then I hear a noise coming from the garage, a few thumps followed by someone yelling, and choose to investigate. Curiously, I make my way through the mudroom. When I push open the door, I find Elliot out there on the drums.

"What is it?" he asks, sweaty, stopping to take a sip of water and stare at me in the doorway. "You look like hell. Did something happen to Diane Sawyer?"

"My mom has someone here to look at The House." I blurt out, and ignore his joke.

"Gross," he says. Then, "Come here."

I make my way over to the drums, and with a serious look, he hands me the sticks.

"What do I do with these?" I say, holding them like they're on fire.

"Have at it," Elliot says, as if it's obvious. "Trust me, it will help."

"But I don't play drums," I say. "I don't play anything."

"Doesn't matter," Elliot says. "That makes it even better."

I hesitate, then sit down at the drum set and reorient my grip until the sticks feel comfortable and light in my palms. And then with one more glance at Elliot, I let the first stick fall against the barrel of the drum, followed by the second stick. They increase in rhythm and intensity until suddenly I am wailing down hard. And when I look back at Elliot one last time he just stands there, arms crossed, grinning from ear to ear.

12

Sorry I'm Late

IT IS so "Will" to show up at school brand spanking new, just months before we all leave forever, and within no time at all host a party more crowded than I could throw after four years.

I walk through his living room and out a set of large doors that open onto a terrace overlooking an expansive pool, where I find him surrounded by friends, dressed in red swim trunks and a T-shirt. His eyes light up when he sees me, and I smile right back. I feel bad about what happened earlier, and I've decided to heed Ava's words. Will is amazing, and okay, so maybe he was written for me. But is that the worst thing in the world?

"Excuse me," he tells nobody in particular, squeezing through and around people to make his way over, his gaze never leaving my face. Without a word, he pulls me into a warm hug, and I can't help but feel safe here. I have never been this girl before. Yes, I have the popular friends, but I've never had the guy.

"Hi," he says with a side smirk as soon as he pulls away. "You look . . ." He doesn't finish his sentence, but instead just shakes his head.

I blush, and look down at the dress Ava picked out for me. It's a dusty rose, with spaghetti straps and buttons down the front. She complained for the zillionth time why I don't own anything with a pattern, and I told her for the zillionth time that patterns are rarely flattering, and never practical.

"Stop," I say to Will, giving him a playful shove. I saw a girl do something like it in a movie. Given my limited experience on how to behave around guys, I've been doing my research.

"I would, but I can't. Bad at lying, remember?" Will says. His pupils are gigantic, and his cheeks are rosy. I'm not sure if it's from me or if he's already a little drunk. "Are you good?"

I open my mouth, trying to find the words. "I've had the weirdest week," I say. "But I think it's about to get better."

Will cocks his head to one side with a small smile. "Do you want something to eat?" he asks, and when I say yes, he takes my hand and leads me through the party to the kitchen.

Spread out on the table is an array of burgers, chips,

guacamole, and—like a prized piece of jewelry in an art museum—a bowl of poke.

"You have poke?" I ask, quickly grabbing a chip so I can scoop some into my mouth. "This is my favorite!"

Will shrugs. "It's decent. I think I added too much salt."

As I bite down on the delicious fish, my eyes light up. "You made this?" I ask when I've stopped chewing.

Will gives me a proud look. "It's my specialty. My grandma's recipe."

Just then Ava wanders in, tugging Navid by the arm. "Hey," she says, stopping and wrapping her arms around Navid's midsection, her head resting just below his collarbone.

That was fast, I think. I don't even know how she does it. But I just grin. "Hey," I say back.

"She has arrived!" Navid grins, straightening his glasses. "We've been waiting for you, Annabelle."

"Did you hear that Will *made* the poke?" Ava looks at me, eyes wide, as though what she's really trying to say is, *Did you hear Will was made for you, and let's all just accept that this is a very good thing.*

"I did," I reply.

"Isn't it so good?" Ava asks.

"It's okay; a little salty, though." I make a face. Then I give Will a big smile.

"Oh, that's it, you're going in," Will says, and grabs me around the waist. I start shrieking and laughing as he pulls me back in the direction of the pool.

"No!" I cry. "No, no, no, please!" Will pulls back for a moment and we look at each other. My arms are around his neck and his beautiful eyelashes are angled down at me. Behind his back, I can see people whispering.

"Okay," he says softly. "Sorry."

"That's okay," I say, and swallow. And then I want to punch myself when, without thinking, I look over my shoulder.

"What are you looking for?" Will asks.

"Nothing." I shrug. "Just seeing who's here."

"Everyone who matters is right here." He smiles, and puts an arm around my shoulders as we head back inside. "You want a beer?"

An hour later, I'm feeling pretty great in Will's kitchen. I don't drink, basically ever, because I don't like the idea of losing control, but I'm letting Ava talk me into it tonight, and Navid and Will. Still, something is gnawing away at my insides, and the beer seems to muffle it, but not with complete success. It keeps rising to the top, from my stomach up to my brain: *Where is Elliot?*

"You're distracted," Ava whispers when Will goes to help with some kind of issue with the music speakers, and Navid gets pulled into conversation with someone from his history class.

"Am I?" I ask. "I thought I was hiding it."

"You can't hide it from me." She sways a bit, but she's okay.

She's already drinking water. "Annabelle, I know you like Elliot. A part of me wonders if maybe you always have. But I'm not sure he's the one. And more important, I'm not sure he's coming."

At this piece of advice, the thing gnawing at my insides seems to wake up a little bit, snore slightly, and then turn over.

"I know," I say, and shrug.

"Have you considered the fact that maybe, yes, in some wild universe Will was made for you. Written for you, every part of him. But maybe even if he wasn't, he'd still, like, be made for you?" she asks. "Have you also considered that maybe your life could be worse than having this incredible guy falling at your feet?"

"The point is that I shouldn't have to consider it," I say. "I shouldn't have to wonder if Will would've made my favorite food on earth either way, or if he just made it because Lucy wrote him to. I don't want to just accept the incredible guy. I want to make my own choices. Can we stop talking about this? You're making my head hurt."

"I'm making my own head hurt," Ava mutters. "But just look at it this way. We don't know where any of this starts or ends. We don't know for sure if it's even happening. We just know Lucy said it is. So maybe Will is perfect for you no matter what! Maybe Lucy's just made it so he behaves more like a dream boy and less like the rest of all these idiots?" She nods over her shoulder to the other side of the kitchen where Navid is arm-wrestling one of his friends on the countertop. Several half-empty beer cans clatter to the floor from their struggle.

I consider this just as Will comes back from the living room and grabs another beer from the fridge. The sight of him makes me smile. But then I hear something else that sends a shiver down my shoulders.

"Sorry I'm late," someone says in a crackly voice, and I turn to find Elliot in the doorway, looking right at me.

"You almost missed the party," I tell Elliot. I'm being cautious, for my own sake and because I am very aware of the fact that over my right shoulder, Will is watching us intently from another part of the terrace. We're leaning on the railing and staring down at the pool.

"I know, I'm really sorry. I can explain," Elliot says.

"It's fine," I say. "It's not like we had set plans." And I'm sure he can explain. But it'll probably be something stupid. Like Lenny, the bassist in his and Sam's band, had people over for beers and he lost track of time. Or he decided to surf too far north in Malibu and got stuck in traffic coming back. It's always the same with him. No responsibility, no problem. Not that I should even care. It's not like he promised me he was coming. It's not like it would matter if he had.

But Elliot is frowning. "No, it's not fine," he says. "It was actually super frustrating. First I got pulled over when I wasn't even speeding."

"Sure," I say with a smile.

"I wasn't, Annabelle," Elliot says more intensely, and my smile disappears. He really is being serious.

"Okay." I nod. "Sorry."

Elliot continues, leaning out over his clasped hands. I've never seen him be so serious. "Then, after I dealt with that, my car broke down. Which was spectacular luck, since my dad keeps those cars in perfect working condition. So I decided to leave it parked on Lincoln, because I was running so late. But when I got out, my phone was just gone. Not in my back pocket, not under a seat—nowhere. It must've fallen out when I got pulled over. So I decided to walk, but I kept getting turned around."

Out in the pool someone does a massive belly flop off the diving board, and the whole party erupts in cheers. I turn my face toward Elliot. This is actually impossible to comprehend. "How do you get turned around in Santa Monica?" I ask. "We've lived here our whole lives, and half of the streets are numbered."

"Thank you for reminding me of that." Elliot makes a face. Then he shakes his head. "I don't know what happened. I can't even believe I made it here. But I made it."

I glance back down at my beer, and when I look up again, I find Elliot looking down, too, but his head is really close to mine. Then he meets my eyes, and my knees feel kind of wobbly.

"If it was so hard to get here, why'd you keep trying?" I eventually ask.

"I think you know why," he says, looking back down.

I swallow. "Because of me?" I ask quietly.

"Would it be okay if it was because of you?" he asks back, just as quiet.

With the tiniest nod, I tell him yes.

I'm still not sure if I believe him, because this story is absurd. But he got here. He still made it. For me, he says. And now that I think about it, I wonder if there is more to his story than I realized.

Elliot's phone rings, and we look at each other.

"So your phone was in your pocket the whole time?" I ask, and start cracking up.

Elliot pulls his phone out of his back pocket, and stares at it like it might bite him. "No, it wasn't," he says slowly.

"Well, apparently it was," I say with a shrug.

"No, it *wasn't*," Elliot says again, firmly. Then he takes the call. "Dad, yeah. I'm so sorry. I swear, I've been treating her like a queen. She's on Lincoln at Wilshire. Can you have Curtis pick her up? Or I can do it in the morning. I know." He runs a hand through his hair. "It was crazy. I promise I was taking good care of her! It was like some unseen force took over the car's engine."

This gives me a small chill. When Elliot hangs up, I study him closely.

"You really did go through all that tonight?" I ask, and my

heart begins to speed up. "The cop, the engine trouble, the phone . . ."

"Yeah." Elliot looks around. "Weren't you here for that story?"

"And you didn't just go home," I say, pushing.

"No, AB," he says, clearly frustrated. "I just told you."

I close my eyes for a moment, trying to get my thoughts straight. It was different before, when it was just about me, about my life. When she was getting in my head. But there's no other explanation for what happened to Elliot tonight. It was *her*. Lucy Keating. She's not just controlling me; she's controlling everything. Elliot having so much trouble tonight. Elliot getting hit on the head with a drumstick at Paper Girl show.

Then the realization hits: Lucy Keating doesn't want Elliot to be close to me.

"I could kill her," I mutter.

"Kill who?" Elliot asks.

"I need a minute," I say, my world spinning, and I carefully make my way out of the room, and up the stairs. I need to think, and there's only one place to do it.

Ten minutes later I'm seated on the toilet seat in Will's immaculately clean, nice-smelling bathroom, my head leaning forward in my hands. So that's it. It's really true. Lucy Keating isn't insane. She is actually writing my life. She didn't just write Will to be perfect. She's writing Elliot to stay away from me.

And now, more than ever, I understand that I don't want Elliot to stay away from me at all.

I think about what Lucy Keating said, about only writing Happy Endings now. As though this was some great gift she was bestowing on all of us. Her readers, her characters. But the fact that in order to do so, she's getting in the way of other possibilities? She is so much more messed up than I ever realized. And I'm not sure there's anything I can do to stop her.

"Okay, Annabelle, think," I say to myself. "You don't get flustered. This isn't you. What do you do whenever a problem arises?"

Suddenly, there's a soft knock at the door.

"Go away, Will," I say.

"It's not Will." Elliot's voice is muffled on the other side of the door, and I sit up straighter, not sure of what to say.

"Are you okay?" he asks. "Annabelle, will you just talk to me?"

I hear my mom's voice in my head. *You've always known what you want, and you've always gone for it without even hesitating.*

So I'm in a book. So Lucy Keating is writing my life. So she thinks Will is the one for me.

Swiftly, I stand up from the toilet seat and smooth down the skirt of my dress.

Who says I can't write my own story?

"Look," Elliot says when I open the door, "I'm sorry if I freaked you out down there. Maybe I shouldn't have told you how hard it was to get here. Or that I came to see you. I understand if that's not what you expected. But I was starting to go insane, and—"

I am barely listening as I pull Elliot inside the bathroom with me. And before I can stop myself, I wrap my arms around his neck.

"What are you doing, Bellybutton?" Elliot asks in a low voice, his eyes becoming heavy lidded.

"Authors can't see characters in the bathroom," I say.

"What are you—?" Elliot starts to ask.

"Later," I tell him, pressing a finger to his lips. And then I kiss Elliot Apfel hard on the mouth. Our lips meet easily, and I feel like I'm being pulled against him by an electric current, my hands reaching up to hold on to the sides of his face as he kisses me back without hesitation.

13

Because I'm with You

IF ELLIOT is surprised when I kiss him, he doesn't show it for very long. Within seconds he drops the empty beer can he's holding and wraps his arms around me, too. And when he pulls away, he rests his head against mine.

"Annabelle," he says with a kind of laugh. Like he's just woken up and seen me there. Like he has things to say but all that he can manage was my name. I don't mind this very much. It turns out the one thing you could do to shut Elliot up is kiss him.

I should be more focused on what I'd just done. I'd kissed my brother's best friend. I'd kissed a person who half the time

I couldn't stand, and genuinely seemed to loathe me in return. I'd kissed someone who wasn't Will, and I'd done it at Will's party. In Will's house.

Elliot leans in and nuzzles my cheek.

But I don't care. Because all of a sudden I realize something: I'd kissed the person I'd wanted to kiss all along. For once, I wasn't thinking about my plan or Lucy's plan. For once I was just doing what I wanted.

"You wanna get out of here?" Elliot voice crackles in my ear.

Things whirl in my mind. What will tomorrow be like? What will people say? Is there even any future here?

Then my eyes meet Elliot's, and they are smoldering. And all that ends up coming out is "Yeah."

I had my bike parked at Will's house, and after we snuck down the back staircase and out the side door, Elliot borrowed another from the garage. I didn't want to see anyone, talk to anyone. Not Will, not even Ava. I didn't want anyone disrupting this perfect moment.

On our way home we stop at a taco shop on Rose Avenue and devour a couple of carnitas as we sit on the edge of the sidewalk. Elliot has his arm draped around my shoulder, and it feels different than it did with Will. With Will it felt good, too, but I was so aware of his presence, about whether he was the right fit for me. With Elliot I don't care how we look to anyone, or what anyone thinks. I just want to listen, to hear his weird stories. This is not about anyone but us.

There is magic in Venice no matter what, but you really feel it at night, especially when you're riding a bike. The streets empty out, and the warm air whips around you as the lamps and patio lights fly by. You think the world is yours. As if you can do anything. As if you could ride your bike to Mexico if you felt like it.

We're almost home, and Elliot rides up ahead, his arms open wide, no hands. I giggle. He loops back and circles around me.

"I like your dress," he says. "Did I tell you that yet?"

"No, but thank you," I say, struggling to keep my tone even as I look straight ahead.

"I like your face," he says, still circling. "Did I tell you that yet?"

"No, but thank you," I say again, and this time I smile.

We stop at a light, and Elliot gets a text on his phone.

"Who is it?" I ask.

"Lenny," he says without responding to the text, and tucks it back in his pants pocket.

"What did he say?" I ask.

"He's at a party, wanted me to stop by."

"Oh," I say, trying to sound easy. "Cool. Did you want to go?"

"Nope," Elliot says.

"Why?" I ask, teasing him, smiling slightly.

The light turns green and Elliot shoots off on his bike.

"Because I'm with you!" he calls back, and my heart swells.

I don't know where we're going, but I follow him down Rose Avenue, right to the beach. Elliot hops off and wheels our bikes across the sand to one of the lifeguard towers. He climbs up through the railing and then offers me a hand. I hop up and sit next to him, and a slight shiver runs through me, even though it's not cold.

Next thing I know an Elliot arm has encircled my shoulders, and my head is resting in that place in his neck, below his chin, where I've been silently dying to be.

Neither of us says anything, and finally I gaze up at him.

He's smiling.

"What?" I ask.

He keeps smiling.

"What?" I ask louder, but I'm starting to smile, too. Not because I get it necessarily, but because he just makes me giddy.

"Well, well, well" is all he says.

"Oh, shut up." I give him a shove.

"I knew you had a thing for me," he squeaks, still laughing, and when I shove him again he grabs my arm and wraps both his arms around me tightly while I squeal.

"I had a thing for *you*?!" I cry in between giggles. "You're the one with the whole *um, uhhh, hey, here I am at a show I know you were already going to.*" I make my voice low like Frankenstein's monster when I say it.

"Oh, is that what I sound like?" Elliot laughs.

"As a matter of fact, you do," I lie.

"Why didn't anybody tell me?" he plays along, pulling back to look at me.

"We all talked about it," I say solemnly. "That's why we're here tonight."

I'm proud of my joke, but Elliot doesn't seem to be listening anymore. He brushes a piece of my hair and tucks it behind my ear.

"I am forever grateful," he says, staring at the lock of hair, then back to my face, and neither of us is laughing anymore.

Even though we've kissed already, even if I'm pretty sure he likes me, looking into Elliot's eyes is hard. But he's holding my gaze, and I kissed him first the last time. So I do the only practical thing possible. I start counting. The first time I hold his gaze for two seconds, then look down at his chest. Then I hold for four seconds. The next time I hold for five, and when I go to glance down again, his lips find mine in a kiss.

This kiss is not like the bathroom kiss, with my awkward pounce, up against the sink with the hair dryer clamoring to the floor. This one is slow and deliberate. It's all Elliot's doing. I am thinking I have never in my life been kissed like this before.

When we finally break away, it's a full hour later, after midnight.

"We need to go," I say.

"I know," he says. "But not yet."

14

Can We Take It All Back?

IT'S STILL dark when I open my eyes, and the stars are sparkling down on us. I glance up at Elliot to find he is wide awake, staring out at the water. He seems calm, the angles of his face still. I run a hand over a cheekbone and up around to his eyebrow, tracing it. I can't believe that, only hours ago, we had never been this close before. I don't want to be any farther away from him than right now ever again.

"You have so many freckles," I tell him. "You don't see just how many until you're up close."

Elliot looks down at me and smiles. Then he says the last thing I expect. "Let's go swimming."

"In what?" I ask as I watch Elliot's smile become a mischievous smirk.

My eyes go wide. "What if we get arrested?" I ask.

"Look around, AB. Nobody is out here right now. And even if they were, what is the worst that could happen? You tell your parents you got arrested for swimming at night? They'd probably be relieved," Elliot says. "You worry too much."

I think on it. He has a point.

"I'll close my eyes." He grins.

"No, you won't." I shake my head.

Elliot shakes his head, too, and I give him a shove.

"I'm kidding!" he yells. "I'm kidding. Of course I will, if that's what you want."

I stare at him, hard, and he stares back, and then I get up and bolt toward the water, shrieking as I begin to strip off the layers, and dive into the ocean in my underwear. It's ice cold, but I'm running on too much adrenaline to care. My whole body feels like it's buzzing.

Behind me I hear a splash, and moments later, Elliot has popped up beside me, nice and close.

"I can't believe you just did that!" he exclaims. "You keep surprising me, AB."

"You really do think I'm some kind of nerd, don't you?" I accuse him as I tread water, kicking my legs below me.

"Well, if the shoe fits." He shrugs, and I respond by splashing him hard in the face. When the water clears the look that remains says I am in big trouble.

"You're going down," Elliot says in a low voice, and moves toward me, his arms encircling my waist. I shriek, but he doesn't splash me or dunk my head below water. His eyes have softened as they search my face.

"I thought I was going down," I say softly, one hand resting on his left shoulder, the other carefully, cautiously, running a hand through his wet hair.

"I changed my mind." His words are barely audible as he leans in close, his lips finding mine in a kiss. This time, despite the chilly water, there is more heat between us. Something chemical that takes my breath away. I wrap my legs around his waist beneath the water as I kiss him back deeply. I wish we could stay out here all night. I wish so very much for this to be my Happy Ending.

"So, not to ruin the moment," Elliot says later, as we sit huddled back in the lifeguard tower, his sweatshirt wrapped around us, "but do we need to talk about Will?"

My heart sinks a little at these words. Will. I don't feel great about what we did tonight. He is a really good guy. Perfect and made for me and possibly highly influenced by Lucy Keating, but still. He didn't deserve me disappearing on him like that.

"What did you want to talk about, specifically?" I say carefully.

"Come on, Annabelle," Elliot says, a little more edge to his voice. "I know you've been spending time with him. Are you just friends? Were you just trying to make me jealous? Or is there more going on there?"

"Make you jealous?" I say. "I'm not one of your band groupies, Elliot."

"Wow, band groupies?" Elliot says. "This isn't the seventies, AB, and also, you didn't answer my question."

"He's a friend," I say.

"Oh, a friend." Elliot's tone is dripping with sarcasm now. This is the Elliot I know. Fiery and irrational. "A friend who just happens to text you all the time, who follows you around all day. Who watched me like a hawk as soon as I showed up to his party, where I find you in *this* dress—"

"I was wearing this dress for *you*," I tell him, even though I haven't been able to admit this to myself until just now.

Elliot doesn't respond; he just looks away, out at the ocean.

I sigh. He doesn't get why this is so confusing. I place a hand at the back of his neck, and gently turn his head toward mine. "There's something I need to tell you. About all of this. About why Will is in my life, and why I think this is all happening."

Elliot furrows his brows together while I take a deep breath and let it all out, the day in Fiction class and what Lucy said to me in the parking lot, about what Ava and I figured out. And it's such a relief to tell him all of this, even if I'm not sure how he's going to take it.

"But you believe me, don't you?" I plead, searching his face. He has to believe me.

Except . . . he doesn't.

Instead, he lets out a long howl of a laugh, and he just keeps laughing.

I don't laugh at all. I can't help it; I'm crushed.

"Take your time," I say dryly. "Get it all out."

"I'm sorry," Elliot says. "But really, Annabelle? Seriously? A crazy woman comes to your class and says she's writing about you, and what? You just believe her?"

"I didn't just believe her," I say. "I thought I just explained that to you." He never really listens, though. "I opened my eyes. To everything that's been happening. All the inconsistencies and the plot twists and—"

"Life is filled with plot twists, Annabelle," Elliot says. "That's what life is."

"Can't you just be sympathetic for a second?" I ask. "My life is not my life. It's all out of my control, and you know how much I like being in control." I say this last part jokingly, because I don't like how this conversation has turned. I want to rewind to ten minutes ago.

But this causes Elliot to think. "It almost feels like some part of you likes this," he says. "Someone leading the way for you. Someone designing your fate. Because every time you do something, like sneak out of a party or like two guys at once, you can have some excuse for it. You're not actually doing anything wrong. It's not really you; it's Lisa Keaton."

"It's Lucy Keating." My blood feels like it's about to boil. There he is, the Elliot I truly know. "And this has been the hardest couple of weeks of my life," I say. "Navigating all of this. I don't enjoy this; I hate it."

"Listen, I get it—your dad's sleeping in the backyard." Elliot nods. "It sucks that they're selling The House, but shit happens. My mom moved away forever, Annabelle. She's not coming back."

I frown, and stare down at my hands, listening to the sound of the waves hitting the beach. "I think this was a mistake," I say quietly. And Elliot is silent for a few moments.

Finally, Elliot shakes his head. He laughs a little then, but it's cold. "I guess this was just an itch that needed scratching."

I feel like I might actually throw up, right here and now, in the dirty Venice sand. An itch? We've know each other forever. Seen each other almost every day for the past sixteen years. And this was just an itch to him? "Well, it sounds like you've figured it out then." I grit my teeth. "I guess you should just go."

Elliot doesn't just go, though. It's three A.M. and the Boardwalk is sketchy enough in bright daylight. So to make matters painfully, awkwardly worse, he insists on seeing me home. Which means fifteen minutes of silent bike riding, neither of us even looking at each other.

As we approach my house, I wonder how we are going to end this evening. I think of all the things I want to say. I'm sorry if I sounded selfish. Or I should've explained sooner. Or if, maybe, when he asked me what the deal was with Will, I had just straight up said, "He's nothing compared to you," which I would've meant. Or maybe just, "Can we take that all back?" Back it all up to just before it all went so very wrong?

I stop my bike and get off, and turn to him, but Elliot's already ridden right past to head home.

15

Sorry!

IT'S TEN A.M., and I'm supposed to be doing my history homework. My calendar tells me—in blue. But for once, I can't bear to think about it. Instead, I am nestled among my fluffy covers, texting with Ava and protesting the rest of the day.

> **Ava:** Navid √. Smooch central.
>
> **AB:** Good work.
>
> **Ava:** Where did you go? Will seemed sad.

AB: Ugh, I was afraid of that.

Ava: Well, it's Will, he didn't really show it, but I could tell. So did you leave with Elliot?

My thumb hovers above the keyboard now.

Ava: Did you KISS ELLIOT?

AB: Well`..`.

Ava: Omgomgomgomgomgomgomg

AB: But it didn't go as planned.

Ava: What do you mean? It wasn't good?

AB: Well, first it was really good. Like amazing. And then`..`. it sort of fell apart. We got into a fight.

Ava: About what?

AB: Lucy. He didn't believe me.

Ava: Well`..`.

AB: I know, I know. But he basically accused me of LIKING someone writing my life.

Ava: Okay but nobody is perfect AB. It's all crazy, no?

I lay my phone down on my chest and consider Ava's words. Outside my windows, the palms stare judgmentally down at me. Maybe I've been focused on the wrong things. If I am real. If Will is real. When the truth is, whether we are all characters or not, it *feels* real. Perhaps that's all that matters. I pick up my phone again.

> **AB:** Okay, fair point. But he was such a JERK about it.

> **Ava:** Well, of course he was. It's Elliot. And I bet you were no peach either.

While I ponder this, another text from her comes through.

> **Ava:** So, now what?

I stare at her words. Now what? And as if on answer, I hear Elliot's laughter erupting from my kitchen, and my heart beats twice as fast.

I say good-bye to Ava and pull on some jeans and a cute sweatshirt, wash my face, apply a little bit of mascara, and try to flounce down the stairs as though I just woke up like this. My brother is facing me, stacking pancakes on three plates. *That was sweet of him*, I think.

But then he says, "Oh, AB, you're here. I figured you'd

already left for the library like usual." And now the third place confuses me.

I know what I have to do next. I have to look Elliot in the eye. I know where he is, I can see his outline sitting on the countertop, his legs moving back and forth. Why is it so hard to face him?

Sometimes the body reacts in ways we can't help, I hear Ava say, and try to prove her wrong.

I lift my head and glance to the right, just in time to see Elliot look away. He stares down at the floor, his brows knitted together.

"Hey, Annabelle," he says dryly. And my stomach flips.

"Hello, Elliot," I say back, my tone flat.

My brother looks up from the pancakes, from me to Elliot. "That's weird," he says.

"What?" Elliot and I both blurt out.

"You never call her by her first name." Sam shrugs.

"So who is the third plate for? Who is stealing my pancakes?" I ask, still standing on the stairs.

Elliot clears his throat. "Whatever," he says. "I don't always call her that." Then finally he casts a look my way, and my rib cage feels like it's trying to squeeze shut.

"Who is the third plate for?" I ask again.

Suddenly, I hear the door to the bathroom open and a familiar voice humming a tune, getting closer to the kitchen, and my limbs start to feel cold.

"Ugh, I am obsessed with that song," the voice says as it gets closer. "You know that one from that band we saw?" she says as she walks into the room, pulling her long, silky hair and throwing it over one shoulder.

Elliot is silent, looking at the floor.

"Come on, guys, you know it," she says to Elliot and my brother. "It's all *hey, girl, something something, can't forget about you.*" Then she stops, and finally notices me.

"Oh, hey, Annabelle," Clara says.

"Hi, Clara," I say back. And I feel like I can't breathe.

One important detail I managed to leave out about Clara, because I don't like to think about her for prolonged periods of time, is that she only speaks in nonspecifics. Like she is too carefree to be bothered. Like she can't listen long enough to learn the name of a street or a band or you know . . . her own bandmate's sister. It took her, I'm not kidding, about ten times of meeting me before she finally got it right, and only because Elliot got mad at her about it.

With Clara, it's always That Thing with the Stuff, That Place with the Food, You Know, You Know, You Know?

Part II, article 16 of *The Elements of Style* reads:

> If those who have studied the art of writing are in accord on
> any one point, it is on this: the surest way to arouse and hold
> the reader's attention is by being specific, definite, and con-
> crete. The greatest writers—

146

Homer, Dante, Shakespeare—are effective largely because
they deal in particulars and report the details that matter.

As I listen to Clara babble on, flipping my own stupid pancakes, I am seriously considering loaning her this book. Or, like, kidnapping her and taping her eyelids open in order to force her to read it. Although, I'm not sure how well she can read.

"It reminds me of, you know, that time we saw that band, when we went to that place? By the beach?" She is sitting next to Elliot at the counter, nestled up against him, trying to run her fingers through his hair. He's tense, I can tell, but what I really can't tell is why. Is it her? Or is it because I am watching?

"What are you talking about, Clare Bear?" my brother asks. He's not annoyed, but he's not overly friendly, either.

"When I walked up to Elliot's car today, he was playing this song over and over. And it just reminded me of the time we drove to that show."

"It was The Kinks, and it was at the Pier, last summer," Elliot says definitively. "The song I was playing was 'She's the One' by Paper Girl. What's your point exactly?"

I almost drop my spatula, realizing that's the song from the concert, when I first felt energy between us, and he got hit with the drumstick. And he was playing it over and over again this morning? That means something, doesn't it? I take a deep breath.

147

"You're mad." Clara pouts at Elliot. "I know you're mad at me, babe. But I already told you: I knew as soon as I left on the tour that it was all wrong. I had to come back to you guys. I had to come back and fix everything." I turn from the stove in time to see her go for Elliot's hair again, and this time he all but ducks.

"Well, maybe we don't need you anymore, Clara," Elliot says.

"Actually, we do kind of need her," Sam says. "While you were off wherever you were last night that you won't tell me about, Trey Olsen approached me at Carter's party. He had someone drop out of opening for Jacuzzi Kill next week and he's asked us to step in."

"Shut up," Elliot says, and high-fives him.

"This is incredible!" Clara squeals.

"You are not a part of this," Elliot says.

"Who else is going to sing, dude?" Sam asks.

Elliot sighs heavily.

"I know you're mad right now, babe," Clara says again, and this time when she rests a hand on Elliot's back, he lets it stay there. "But I'm here. And sooner or later you're going to have to accept that."

At this point I can't take it anymore. I walk out into the front yard, leaving my pancakes to burn, and bury my face in my hands, smoothing out my eyebrows to de-stress, a technique we learned in gym class. This is all wrong. This is not what was supposed to happen. Why is Lucy Keating doing this?

"Isn't this enough?" I say out loud. "You've got your drama and your intrigue! You even got your sexy midnight swim! Can't you just say the story is over?"

I hear the sound of a little biplane passing overhead, and drop my hands to look up. Written across the sky in big, loopy, letters is:

Sorry!

16

Is It That Kind of Book?

ANXIETY NEVER used to be something I was particularly familiar with. At least, not until this whole literary fiasco happened. When problems arise, I usually just handle them. I never understand when I see classmates in the library in tears because they have a paper due they aren't even close to finishing. How did they get there? They knew when their deadline was. Why didn't they just make the time?

I have to admit, though, this whole thing with Lucy Keating has set me off my game, because you can't be prepared for things you didn't see coming. Epstein taught us all about act structure and character arcs, the highs and lows a protagonist must go through to reach the resolution to their conflict.

"Not every novelist does this, but Lucy writes her books with distinct act breaks," she told us in class the other day. "So did Shakespeare. At the end of Act One, the characters learn of their debacle—i.e., Romeo and Juliet learn their families are sworn enemies. The next low would be when they think they are going to have happily ever after, but something awful happens, like when Mercutio dies. At the end of the Act Two high, Romeo and Juliet have hatched a plan to run away together and we think it's going to work. Hooray!" She pumped her fist into the air. "The third act low is the lowest low, the most dramatic—i.e., the death of the two characters. Does that make sense?"

It did make sense, back in the classroom. And it was also really interesting. Now, sitting in my bedroom at home, after the Clara run-in in my kitchen, it's a huge pain in my butt. How am I expected to function when I don't even know where I am in my story? The moment Elliot and I kissed, I actually thought, *This could be my Happy Ending*. But what if we aren't even at the midpoint? How many highs and lows do I have to go? And am I supposed to give Will a shot, knowing full well someone is writing us to be together?

And so, I know what I have to do. That is, in this case, I must do nothing. Literally. I've decided not to leave my room until I have this whole thing under control. After all, if I can't leave my room, I can't really do anything interesting. And who wants to read a book about someone who doesn't do anything?

"So you've got this totally under control?" Ava says on my front lawn when she stops by to pick up my phone. If I don't have a phone, I can't be texted. By Will or Elliot. And if I can't be texted, I can't flirt or fight or even chat. Eventually, she'll have to give up on this story and we'll see how things really are, right?

"Totally under control," I say with a confident nod.

"And totally under control to you means hiding in your room until Monday?" Ava says.

"Whatever gets the job done." I shrug.

Ava gives a small military send-off. "Godspeed," she says, and hops on her bike to go meet Navid at the beach.

Things aren't going totally to plan, however. For one thing, it's only been eight hours, and I'm losing my mind. I've finished all my homework for the following week, and reorganized my bedroom twice. Now I'm just curled up in my bed, watching my secret vice, the thing that always relaxes me when it's too rainy to run, or I'm sick or injured: It's a reality TV show where fifteen amateur baking contestants from the United Kingdom compete against one another at an old English estate for the title of master baker and a grand prize.

Something about the diligence with which they measure out their dry ingredients, the smoothness of the pastry, and the jovial way they conduct themselves in such a competitive environment sets me at peace with the world.

A few hours later, I have just finished my fourth episode in a row when there is a heavy knocking on my door.

I shoot up out of bed like a character in a bad spy movie. "Who is it?" I call out.

"Your brother," Sam says. "Let me in."

"No," I reply.

"Why not?" he asks.

"Are you alone?" I shoot back.

"What? Of course I'm alone!" He sounds exasperated. "Who would I be with?"

Elliot, I think, *obviously*. But I keep the thought to myself.

"Okay, I have better things to do than stand outside your door all day, but Mom says if you don't come down for dinner, the world will end," Sam says.

"Is it that kind of book?" I whisper. That thought hadn't even occurred to me. Lucy is a romance writer. Beach cottages and European vacations, Manhattan love stories. But what if she is taking a departure into new territory beyond Happy Endings. What is next? Zombies?

I throw the door open.

Sam is just standing there watching me, a puzzled look on his face. "Sometimes I wonder if one of us was adopted," he says. "And by one of us, I mean you. Come down to dinner. It's fish tacos, your favorite. Dad made the guac, too." He starts jogging down the stairs, and then stops.

"Were you with Elliot last night?" he asks.

I swallow. "How'd you hear about that?"

"Someone saw you guys on your bikes."

I nod. "Yeah, we rode home together from a friend's party," I say, as though explaining the logistics will hide the more significant details. The fact that we then went to the beach, and oh, that we totally made out for hours, then got in a massive fight and now Clara is back.

Sam's jaw moves back and forth. "Not like Elliot to hit up a Cedar Spring party, especially not these days," he observes, watching me carefully.

"Yeah, I guess he felt like he should give it a shot or something, before we all graduate." The words come out too quickly, and I immediately wish I could take them all back.

"Be careful, AB," Sam says. "You and Elliot are really . . . different. Just watch yourself." Sometimes I think of my brother as just some kind of big bear who lives in my house, never puts the seat down, and chews his cereal too loudly. But the truth is, he sees me much more clearly than I realize.

"Careful with what?" I ask, playing dumb.

"Don't play dumb," Sam says, and I am no longer playing dumb. I am dumb. "Neither of us wants to have this discussion, so let's just keep it brief. Elliot is my best friend, but he's terrible with girls. Just be careful."

"I wasn't even—" I start to say, but Sam has already reached the bottom of the staircase.

My shoulder slump, and with a sigh, I head back into my room. Sam only knows the half of it. What would he say if he really knew what was going on?

I lie back down on my bed. If all this is really happening, what do I expect to happen next? For the baking show host to reach out of the screen and offer me some cake? This is not like me. I am above all things a rational human being. I shake myself, go to my mirror, and run a comb through my hair, then notice how flushed my cheeks are, and decide it's finally time to open a window.

No sooner than I do, however, the strangest thing happens. A paper airplane flies softly through the window and lands directly on my desk. I approach it delicately, as though it's an explosive device or a potentially dangerous animal.

But as soon as I unfold the airplane, my blood runs cold. Written in typewriter font on a piece of delicate white paper is the following line:

Just then Will knocked on Annabelle's door, bringing her exactly what she needed.

"Oh, you have got to be kidding me," I say. And a moment later, I hear it. A set of knuckles softly hitting my bedroom door. *Tap tap tap.*

"Annabelle?" I hear Will say.

I sigh, and consider pretending I'm not in here.

"I know you're in there," Will says. "Your brother told me when he let me in."

I roll my eyes, then open the door. But there is no Will there. There is a Will hand, and it's holding a giant waffle cone, one perfect scoop of Oreo ice cream nestled in the middle.

Will steps into frame. "You're alive!" He smiles.

"I'm alive," I say, trying to hide how tired I feel.

"You haven't been answering my texts," he says, unfazed by my less than hospitable welcome.

"I don't have my phone," I explain. *A lot of good that did.*

Will gives me a look. He should hate me right now. I disappeared from his party with another guy, and I haven't even bothered to explain. But instead he says, "Don't be difficult, Annabelle. Let me feed you. You and I both know that ice cream makes it all better."

Reluctantly, I take the ice cream cone, and let Will into my room. By this point I've gotten used to seeing Elliot in here, sprawled out on the couch, his arms tucked behind his head. But Will looks out of place. He seems nervous about where to look or where to sit.

"So this is the top-secret lair of Miss Annabelle Burns," he says, placing his hands in his pockets and looking around.

"This is where the magic happens," I reply.

"Nice bookshelf," he observes, wandering over to it. "How'd you arrange it? Alphabetical?"

"Right now it's by genre," I explain, feeling embarrassed.

Will nods. "Mine is currently arranged by author's first name."

This should impress me, should make me swoon, and a week ago it would have, like the car organizer did. But by now I know it's all a farce. None of it means anything.

If Will senses the tension, he chooses to push through it. "Then, of course, I have a whole section for my comic books," he adds.

"You read comic books?" I blurt out in surprise.

"Only my whole life. Why?" Will seems surprised right back.

"You just don't strike me as the type," I say.

"If that's how you feel, then you haven't read many comic books," Will tells me. "They aren't all superheroes and villains. Though . . . there is a lot of that. Maybe I can show them to you sometime."

"I'd like that," I say, and I mean it.

"So what happened to you last night?" Will switches topics, and it catches me off guard. He's looking at me sincerely now. I consider telling him the truth, that Elliot and I kissed, but what's the point? It's not like I'm going to be with Elliot anyway. It's not like anything's really going to change as long as Lucy Keating is running the show.

"I wasn't feeling well, so Elliot took me home. Sorry we borrowed your bike. I can drop it off whenever you want."

"I don't care about the bike, Annabelle. I care about you." It's romantic. Epically so, in fact. But does it really mean anything?

I take a breath. "Will . . . why are you here?"

"What do you mean?" he asks.

"You're right; I didn't tell you. I just left your party, without saying good-bye. It was rude. And yet, here you are with an ice cream cone." I'm pushing him to think about it. To consider, for a moment, if this is even what he really wants.

Will shrugs. "You haven't eaten any of it, by the way." He points to the cone in my hand.

Slowly, and just for show, I scoop a big bite up with my tongue.

Will watches me while I chew, and waits for me to swallow. "And?" he asks.

I smile, and actually feel a laugh coming on.

"I knew it," he says.

"You're weird," I say.

"I know," he says back, and surprises me again with what comes next. "So nothing is going on with you and Elliot? I'm asking for a friend." He smiles, all charm, and it's as if he's some kind of CIA operative, and the ice cream cone is part of his interrogation tactic. But this time, I don't have to lie. I think about Clara's hand on Elliot's shoulder at breakfast and take another big bite of my cone.

"No," I say finally through my chews. "Nothing is going on with me and Elliot."

17

You Think I'm Cute?

WILL HALE is taking me on another honest-to-goodness date. It's not a casual hang. It's not a "What are you up to now?" or a "I heard you needed a ride home," or a "Hey, do you want to leave this party together and go kiss on the beach?" He planned it all. Every single step. And this time, Elliot won't be around to ruin it.

"I realized I was going about it all wrong," Will said when he called me on Sunday, after I got my phone back from Ava. "I've been trying too hard to figure you out. Instead, I should share something with you about *myself*, but since I just moved here, I don't really have a lot to show."

So he decided the most efficient thing to do would be to create a list of five awesome things I have never done in LA, even though I've lived here my entire life.

"Chances are I won't have done them, either, so we can be fish out of water together. We can have a completely unique experience!" he announced. He actually emailed me an online survey for it, titled *Annabelle & Will's Unique Experience*. He would make the plan; I just had to check off the boxes.

And right now that plan has landed me one hundred and thirty feet above the Santa Monica Pier, and God knows how many feet above the ocean, on the Pacific Wheel.

"It's the only solar-powered Ferris wheel in the world," Will informs me as I gaze at the views of the Pacific coastline. There's a slight breeze today, and it feels good, warm air whipping around my skin. I close my eyes and bask in the sun on my face.

"Interesting," I say.

"Are you impressed that I know that?" I hear Will ask, his tone teasing.

"So impressed," I tease back. "What else do you know?"

"Where should I begin?" He laughs, and I giggle.

"Seriously, though, I play a mean game of trivia. Ask me anything. I know every state capital."

"Oh, really?" I say, suddenly interested. I open my eyes and look at him. "Okay, Illinois."

"*Oooo*, toughie." Will nods. "I see what you're trying to do there. You think I'll say Chicago, don't you? Well, nice try. It's Springfield. I wasn't born yesterday."

"Impressive." I cross my arms as we circle around, the crowd on the Pier swarming below us. To be honest, the Santa Monica Pier freaks me out a little bit. From a distance, it's a wild, quirky landmark. Up close, it's filled with hot and sweaty tourists, and a variety of characters that range from humorous to downright frightening, like the a guy covered in head-to-toe tattoos, barely an inch of his real skin visible. "How'd you get so good at facts like this?" I ask, trying not to think about it.

"I just have a knack for it," he says. "I think I may have a photographic memory. Also"—he makes a face—"I wasn't very cool growing up." He makes little quotation marks around the word *cool*, and I resist telling him there's nothing very cool about that hand motion. But regardless, what he just said surprised me.

"Seriously?" I ask, then I correct myself. "Sorry. It's just that's kind of hard to believe." Not only is Will movie-star handsome, he gets along with everyone. It's impossible to picture him not fitting in.

Will shrugs. "My body took a while to grow into itself. I was all gangly limbs and no body fat, my hair was really big, my pants were always too short, and as if that wasn't enough, I was kind of a know-it-all. Always correcting other people. I didn't have a lot of friends. Hence the comic book obsession." He casts me a wary look. "Should I not have told you that?"

"It explains a lot, actually," I say.

"Really?" Will laughs. "I'm that much of a jerk, huh?"

"No, no," I say, resting a hand on his forearm when I say it, and Will looks down at his arm like I've just turned it into gold. "It makes sense that you weren't super-cool."

"Somehow this isn't getting any better." Will makes another face.

Now I am laughing and trying to explain through my giggles. "It's just that you are, like, *you*. You know?"

"I don't know." The corner of Will's mouth turns up.

"Don't make me say it," I whine.

"Enlighten me." Will rests his hands behind his head.

I roll my eyes. "You're cute and charming. And everyone likes you. But you're not a jerk. You've had to earn it. I'm just saying it makes a lot of sense."

Will doesn't say anything for a moment; he just smirks at me.

"*What?*" I finally say.

"You think I'm cute?" is all he asks, as the chair blows back and forth in the wind.

After the Ferris wheel, we have lunch at the trendiest restaurant in Beverly Hills, laughing the whole time at how over-the-top fancy it is, how many forks there are to eat with, and the French poodle sitting next to us in an actual chair. Then we follow a star map to all the most absurd mansions on Sunset Boulevard, and even manage to get onto one of the properties before a gardener wielding giant pruning sheers kicks us out. We catch a comedy show in Beachwood Canyon, and end the day watching *ET* at the Hollywood Bowl, while the LA Philharmonic plays along as the soundtrack. It's a perfect night, and the stars are twinkling above us. And Will planned every single detail of it for me.

"Hey," I tell him as we walk out of the venue to his car.

"Hey what?" he asks, gazing down at me.

"Thank you for this day. It was pretty awesome."

In response, Will just smiles, and carefully takes my hand in his. "Don't mention it," he says, and holds my hand the rest of the way. And I let him.

When Will drops me off that night, I walk in to find the downstairs bathroom seems to have exploded all over the living room. Cabinet doors and pieces of tile lay on every surface, and the toilet is next to the sofa.

My mom comes in from the kitchen, wielding Napoleon like a weapon.

"Why is there a toilet next to the sofa?" I ask.

My mother sets down Napoleon carefully, but he starts growling, so she picks him up again, rolling her eyes. "It needed an upgrade," she says.

"Did it really?" I ask. "Everything was working just fine."

"Don't start with me, Annabelle," she says. "It needed an upgrade for potential buyers."

"Don't *start* with you?" I blurt out. "Like any of this has any-thing to do with me?" If I'm correct, a lot of this is being done *to* me.

"I have a lot on my plate, AB," my mother says. "Managing my own projects while trying to get this place in order. Then there is the stuff with your father, which I won't talk to you about, because it's none of your business. I don't want to have this discussion with you anymore. We are selling The House, and that's that. There are other people affected by this situa-tion, you know."

I'm kind of taken aback by this. Then I think that I spend so much time wanting my parents to treat me like an adult, and when they do, I get annoyed by it, and that's not fair.

"I'm sorry," I say. "I know I am not the center of the universe. I know this all must be very hard for you."

My mother sighs and gives me a hug as Napoleon growls gently between us. "Thank you for saying that. Now, if you don't mind taking the general, I have to go take the trash out."

I am just turning to head up the stairs with Napoleon when Sam and Elliot burst through the back door, all loud voices and laughter.

"Oh, hey," Sam says to me. He gives an awkward glance at Elliot, but doesn't say anything.

Elliot just stands there, watching me. He lifts a hand in the air, a silent *hi*.

"Hey," I say back. "I was just heading upstairs. Try to keep the music to a minimum, if you don't mind. I have a lot of work to catch up on."

But twenty minutes later, I am doing no work at all, because I finished it already. I'm lying in my bed staring at the ceiling, feeling sad and confused. Confused as to how Will could make me feel so warm and happy on our date, and how one silent hand gesture from Elliot could make me feel completely alone.

Napoleon appears in the doorway, eyeing me.

"Can I help you?" I ask.

I follow his small, scraggy body as he makes delicate steps across the carpet, and then, after a deliberate pause, launches himself at the duvet.

Given that I have never seen him do anything of this nature before, I resolve to wait this out. And, like the miracle of a baby that is walking for the very first time, Napoleon tiptoes over my legs, and settles gently down on my blanket-covered stomach, rolling himself into a tight little ball and exhaling an audible sigh.

My eyes stay locked on Napoleon, once my mortal enemy, and I'm at a complete loss for what to do. I once resolved to hate him from the bottom of my soul, but the feeling of his little body resting on mine soothes me. Some small voice inside me wonders . . . can he tell I'm upset? Is Napoleon actually trying to make me feel better? I push it from my mind, but it still makes me think: Perhaps we are all capable of change.

18

What If I Don't Know What I Want?

"YOU'RE GETTING better." Epstein gives an encouraging nod as she slaps our latest assignment down on my desk on the following Monday morning. "You're not quite there yet, but whatever you're doing, keep doing it."

I glance at the letter written at the top of the page. *B+*. It's about a full grade below what I usually get in my other classes, but in Fiction, it's a start. If only I knew what got me here. I had a hard time making sense of everything after Clara showed up on Saturday, and nothing seemed to do the trick, so I ended up writing about it. Before I knew it, I was examining three perspectives. Me, coming down the stairs to face Elliot after our fight; my brother, cooking pancakes obliviously; and Elliot, sitting on the countertop, with two girls he had kissed in the same room.

And yes, I refused to give Clara a perspective. She hardly has a point of view as it is.

It bugs me that Elliot may have gotten me this B. Aside from that awkward moment with my brother, I haven't talked to him since that morning. He reached out, once. He sent me some useless Van Morrison song, and "we should talk," but I didn't listen to it, and I'm not ready to talk. I don't know what there is to say.

And besides, now that Clara's back, I can only assume they are also back together. Or will be soon. I don't need him to tell me that. I already know. I am Annabelle, who color-codes her calendar. And she is Clara, who speaks in nonspecific. And he is Elliot, who hates to be put in a box. Guess which girl is the better fit?

"Ms. Epstein?" I ask. "I have a question."

Like many of my teachers, Epstein is wary of me. She had me for sophomore English, and she understands my questions are sometimes complicated, and that I am not easily satisfied, that with one question often comes three to four follow-ups. Even someone as passionate about her work as Epstein can find it tiring.

"Must we today, Annabelle?" Epstein sighs.

"I'm afraid we must," I say solemnly.

"Fair enough, go ahead," Epstein says, settling in, and leans her head against her fist.

"I know you talked to us a little bit about act structure the other day, and the highs and lows. But how does a writer know what those are, exactly? When you're making it all up, how does it not become some kind of jumbled, tangled mess?"

To my surprise, Epstein nods. "It's a great question, as usual, Annabelle." She gets up and takes a place at the board.

Margot raises her hand. "Will this be on the test?" she asks.

"There are no tests in this class, only your final project." Epstein doesn't even bother turning from the board to answer.

"Then why do we take notes?" Margot says stubbornly.

At this, Epstein does turn around. "To learn something," she says curtly. "Now as I was saying. When you're writing a book, or even just a story, you don't just arbitrarily choose your character, your time, your place. You need to understand your purpose. What are you really trying to say?" She writes the word *character* on the board, and taps it once with her whiteboard marker. "You need to understand you're what's driving them, what their hopes and dreams are. Many believe the best characters are those whose wants contrast directly with their needs. And that juxtaposition, the obstacles the character must face and the highs and lows they encounter while getting there, is what drives the plot." Beneath *character*, Epstein has written *drive, needs, wants*.

"But what if I don't know what I want?" I ask, exasperated, and then realize I sound ridiculous. And also, Epstein isn't the person I'm angry at.

"I mean, it all just seems so contrived," I cover. "I thought authors wrote organically, let things come to them. I didn't realize it was all so . . . formulaic."

Epstein mulls this over for a moment. "I hear what you're saying," she says. "But look at it this way. It's for our benefit, our enjoyment. What you probably don't realize is that as a reader, a viewer, you come to expect these highs and lows. You look forward to them. And in some cases, if you didn't get them, you'd lose interest."

Epstein goes about splitting us into groups to discuss our favorite books and movies and the narrative arcs within them.

I stare at my notebook for a few minutes, tapping my pencil against the desk. Then I look across the room where Will is dutifully participating in a group discussion, gesticulating with a smile as the other members of his group lean on their elbows making googly eyes. I'm not the only character in this room. We all are. And maybe, for once, it wouldn't be so bad to just accept the *want* that Lucy Keating has created for me.

I am just grabbing my calculus book out of my locker the next day, when suddenly the usual math equations turn into words:

"I was thinking of going to the library" I hear in my ear now, and notice Will has indeed snuck up next to me.

"Thanks for letting me know," I say with a small smile, also not looking at him, and trying to tune out the narrative in front of me.

"I was thinking it would be more enjoyable if you were also there," he adds.

I smile bigger, still not making eye contact. "I was going to swing by the paper, but I could probably arrange that," I tell him.

"Excellent . . ." Will leans in closer. "Do you think, if it's not too much trouble, you could also arrange to hold my hand?"

"I think I could probably arrange that also," I say back as we make our way up the stairs to the library.

And I do.

19

That Was Sarcasm

"DID I see Will Hale holding your hand this morning?" Lee asks at lunch that day. I look up, eyes wide, and the whole table inhales in one collective gasp.

"Oh my God," Ava says. "She did. She told me at first period and I didn't believe her."

"It's nothing," I say, mixing my fruit yogurt about twenty stirs more than necessary. It's beginning to look like pink-flecked whipped cream.

"It's not nothing," Nisha says.

"He is such a smoke show!" Lee shakes her head like she can't believe his hotness.

"So you're dating him?" Ava asks. "Why didn't you tell me?"

"I'm not dating him. We haven't even kissed," I say. "We're just spending time together."

"If I was *spending time with him,* I would take out an ad on television to make sure the world knew," Nisha says, raising her eyebrows as she spears a piece of lettuce on her fork.

Before I can respond, I look up and watch as Elliot strides in our direction, his eyes locked on me the whole way.

"Oh, boy," Ava mutters.

"Remember when Annabelle had no love life to speak of?" Nisha whispers, chewing on a piece of carrot.

"Ladies," Elliot calls as he approaches the table.

"Elliot," my friends mumble disdainfully.

"Annabelle," he says.

"Elliot?" I say expectantly.

"You've been ignoring me," Elliot says.

"I've been ignoring *you*?" I ask. "You didn't even speak to me at The House yesterday."

"That's because you never responded to my text. And you didn't speak to me, either."

"A YouTube video of Van Morrison live in concert does not exactly count as reaching out," I tell him. My friends shoot one another wide-eyed glances.

Elliot sighs. "Can we talk somewhere in private?" he asks.

"Anything you want to say to me you can say in front of them," I say stubbornly.

"No, I know I can; I just don't want to." Elliot crosses his arms in front of his chest, his demeanor hardening. And then he says nothing. Neither do I. We stare at each other for a solid sixty seconds before I finally break.

"Oh my God, *fine*," I say, standing up, my heartbeat picking up and this weird tingling sensation creeping up my neck. Elliot has on worn black jeans and a blue T-shirt with a chest pocket. He looks pretty hot. I start packing my stuff.

"You haven't finished your lunch." He points at the food in front of me.

"I'm not hungry," I say, picking up my tray.

Elliot's shoulders fall.

"Come on, Annabelle, can't we just talk?"

I set my tray down and shrug. "Okay," I say. "Talk."

Elliot shuffles his feet for a second. "I would like you to come to my show on Friday night. I'm asking in advance. Not as an excuse. I genuinely want you to be there. I . . ." He casts a look back at my friends before leaning close to me. "I just really want you to be there. Okay?"

I exhale out of my nose as I look over his face, his brows knitted together, his bottom lip tucked under his front teeth. He's trying.

"I'll think about it," I say.

"I can live with that," he replies.

I nod, and then, because I don't feel like standing here next to him any longer, I turn to go. A million thoughts swim in my head. The fact that I shouldn't go, but I want to. The fact that I held Will's hand this morning, but Elliot still has a power over me I can't explain.

"I know you can hear me," I say to Lucy out loud. "I know this is the point of a love triangle, but it still sucks."

I open my locker and a note falls out on turquoise paper. *Poor you*, it says in scrawling cursive. And a few lines below: *That was sarcasm.* At the top, in beautiful calligraphy, it reads FROM THE DESK OF LUCY HARRISON KEATING.

20

Animal Man

I'M JUST wrapping up a newspaper meeting at the end of the school day when Will knocks gently on the doorframe.

"Are you busy?" he asks, before nodding to Hector in greeting.

I look at Hector, who is waiting to discuss next week's layout. "Are you cool to wait a couple minutes?" I ask.

"No problem," he says. "I'm gonna go grab a soda from the vending machine. Looks like this may be a late one tonight."

When we're alone, Will runs a hand through his hair. He seems nervous. "I have something to run by you, but I'm genuinely concerned you might think I'm crazy," he says.

"Try me," I say over my shoulder, as I make one last note on the dry-erase schedule. Because nothing surprises me these days.

"Okay, I'll tell you, but you're definitely going to think I'm crazy when I tell you we can only discuss it in the bathroom," he replies. Slowly, I cap the marker I was using, and set it down on a table. I have a feeling I know what's coming.

A few moments later, I am sitting on the sink of the single-person handicapped bathroom, and Will stands in front of me, wielding a comic book. I realize Hector is probably going to think we are making out in here, but I don't care.

"So, I'm not quite sure where to begin," Will says. "That first day in class when we met Lucy Keating, I couldn't figure out what you were so upset about. It seemed really out of character for you, a straight-A student and a *writer*, to struggle so much with Fiction. But then I got to know you, and I understood. Lucy had described your life. The reason I was late to class that day wasn't because I was late. I was nervous. I was waiting outside the whole time, and I heard her. So then I started secretly reading her books. And I couldn't help but think about how odd it was. How familiar. My family moving here on such short notice at such a dramatic time, senior year. The way I . . ." He looks down for a second. "The way I felt the moment I first saw you. Like I'd been struck by lightning."

I blush.

"I thought I was overthinking the whole thing. Being crazy about someone will convince you of anything. But then I was reading one of my comic books." He holds it out to me. On the cover is a superhero-looking guy in a leather jacket, '80s shades, and what appear to be no pants.

"Where are his pants?" I ask.

Will pauses, surprised, and looks at the cover again. "He's wearing pants. His leggings are orange. I can understand the mistake, actually." He stops and shakes his head. "But that's not the point!"

"Sorry!" I say, flipping through some pages. "Please, continue."

Will points at the cover. "I've been really into the story of this guy Animal Man, who was created, like, half a century ago, but has been revived again in the last twenty years. Comic book writers sometimes send weird, meta messages in their work, but as I just learned, Animal Man is one of the most notorious, blatant uses of this. In Animal Man, the main character actually begins to discover he is a character in a comic book. And he meets the comic book writer himself."

He flips to a page and opens it, and I feel like I'm experiencing déjà vu. In the scene, a man in a sweater is telling Animal Man that he's written his life, and he points to words on a computer screen that describe everything that is happening around them.

"Holy shit," I said. "So much for being original."

Will's big eyes are staring at me intently as he speaks, his words coming out quickly. It's so amazing that he's figured this out all by himself, when Elliot wouldn't even consider the idea when I told him face-to-face. In making Will a recovering comic book addict with a wild curiosity, Lucy Keating may have just created a monster.

Will is still talking. "It's true, isn't it? I read that, and I got sincere goose bumps thinking about your interaction with Lucy in class that day. And I know this is all crazy, but it also feels weirdly right. And I have a feeling you already know that," he says.

I take a deep, slow breath, and then slowly, I nod.

"You did," he says, more of a statement than a question.

"I did," I say finally.

"I knew it!" Will yells, and I shush him. He puts his hands in his hair and leans his head back toward the ceiling. "This is nuts," he finally says.

"You have no idea," I say.

"How long have you known?" he asks.

I think for a moment. "She told me that day in the parking lot. But I didn't totally believe her until—" I pause. *Until I realized I wanted to kiss both you and Elliot. Until Elliot got lost in Santa Monica. Until I realized Lucy Keating was trying to give me a Happy Ending I didn't want*, I want to say next. "Until the night of your party," I say instead.

And then I tell him everything. The changes in eye color, in the ice cream, the rain, staying up all night in Rosewood Café & Bookstore. I tell him everything except the parts about kissing Elliot. But I tell him a little bit about that, too, about the love triangle. About Elliot getting hit on the head with the drumstick, and about how hard it was for him to get to Will's party that night. Will is quieter during those moments.

"I'm not thrilled to be a part of this love triangle," he says. "But I guess it's the nature of the beast."

"I appreciate that," I say.

"And besides, I intend to fight for you like hell, so I'm not really worried." He grins, and even if only a few hours ago my mind was filled with Elliot, I smile, too.

But an hour later, after my meeting with Hector, Will still isn't satisfied. I find him waiting in the hallway, his hair messier than usual, and his usually perfect button-down all wrinkly.

"I just have so many questions," he says as he drives me home. "I keep thinking, what is real and what isn't? What of my decisions are really mine at all?"

"Welcome to the club. It's best not to think at all," I say dryly, adjusting the radio.

"Like maybe I don't even—" Will starts.

"Maybe you don't even like me?" I cut in, but Will's face goes dark.

"No, I definitely like you; I never doubted that for a minute," he says. "I actually was thinking, maybe I'm not such a good guy after all."

At this I snort through my nose. "You are the *'goodest'* guy of all," I tell him.

"But maybe I'm not!" he exclaims as we stop at a light. "Maybe I am because she made me that way. What would happen if I broke the rules? Step outside myself? Sometimes I feel like quite literally I can do no wrong. But what if I could, if she'd just let me?"

"Well, maybe you should try," I tell him. "Try to break the rules and see how it goes. I haven't quite figured it out yet, but I think there's a way."

"Yeah." Will nods, staring off, his mind clearly somewhere else. "Yeah, I'm sure there is. We just have to know where to find it."

21

Today Was a Good Day

I'VE JUST aced a pop quiz in history class the next day when Dr. Piper pops her shiny-haired head in and whispers something to Mr. Ober before both cast a glance my way.

Silently, I point a finger to my chest and mouth *Me?*

They both nod.

"It's nothing serious," Piper assures me as she walks me to the front doors of the main building, her heels click-clacking the whole way, her hips swaying from side to side. "Your father said it's his mistake: He thought he booked the tickets to your great-grandmother's ninetieth birthday for *tomorrow*, Friday, but he actually booked a day early by accident, so you all have to rush to the airport."

I nod, thinking in my head that neither of my grandmothers is older than eighty-two. But if there's one person in the world I don't mind deceiving, it's Piper, and I'm curious about what's going to happen next. It's interesting that she's not the least bit suspicious. I bet she'd never let Elliot get away with something like this.

"There's a car outside waiting to take you to the airport," she says, and when we open the front door, sure enough, a black Escalade is waiting. This continues to mystify me, since my father hates paying for even a taxi to the airport. I saw him and my mom take a black car once, to a reunion screening of his TV show, but only because she had insisted.

"Come on," she'd said, wrapping her arms around his tuxedo shoulders when it rolled up, while she herself looked stunning in a sophisticated black gown. "Live a little." They both grinned at each other. Thinking of the memory now makes my heart ache.

"Thanks so much for understanding, Dr. Piper," I say, shaking her hand, and walk out the doors with the feeling like I am a cast member of *Ferris Bueller's Day Off*.

Then, once she's safely out of sight, I hesitantly open the door to the SUV and peer inside.

Seated at the wheel is a familiar face, and it's grinning.

"What are you doing?" I ask.

"Breaking the rules," Will says, and he looks like he's never been prouder of anything in his whole life.

Sunset Boulevard, just west of Doheny, is one of my favorite drives in LA. The road slopes in and around, up and down, passing high gates and the occasional giant home that's out in the open for all to see. Will and I came up this way the other day on our Tour of the Stars, but it never gets old. This time we are taking it all the way to the ocean. Will explains the car belongs to his father.

"Midlife crisis car. I took it to school this morning, then faked sick, and called in the excuse."

"Why?" I ask.

"Because I want to prove Lucy Keating wrong!" he exclaims. "I want to make our own rules. She isn't running our lives, Annabelle. She can't. Today, *we* decide."

Just then a text comes through on my phone. It's Elliot.

Are you coming to the show?

I watch the little bubbles move for about a minute, curious as to what he will say next, but then the bubbles stop altogether. I exhale.

"Game on," I say to Will, and shut my phone off.

Will wants to get as far away from our world as possible, so we head for northern Malibu, and stop at the Malibu Country Mart to get provisions. It's one of my favorite places to go for lunch. Barrels full of any kind of chip you like, a wall full of candy, and sandwiches that make your mouth water. It's only on our way out that I notice the cookies.

"Those are the size of my head!" I exclaim.

"So take one," Will says.

I look at the line, wrapping around the interior shop. "It'll take too long. Not worth it," I say.

"No, Annabelle," Will says, his tone becoming conspiratorial. *"Take one."*

My eyes go wide. "We're exhibiting free will! Not stealing!" I protest.

"It's one cookie, Annabelle!" Will whispers. "They make it for fifty cents and sell it for six dollars. I'm guessing you've never even stolen a piece of dental floss before. So just do it."

I swallow, take a deep breath, then quickly tuck the giant cookie under the sweater I'm holding.

We take off running for the car, and I let out a squeal the whole way. I can't remember the last time I felt so exhilarated. I split the cookie open, and we each take a huge bite.

"*Mmm*, tastes like rebellion." Will chuckles between chews. I laugh harder.

We keep driving up the coast, the houses getting farther and father apart, no longer lining the western side of the Pacific

Highway. Instead there are farm stands, dunes, and bushes filled with pink flowers. When we arrive at the beach parking lot twenty minutes later, Will is just about to pull his credit card out to pay for parking at the kiosk, but I stop him.

"What if you don't?" I say.

"But we have to." Will frowns.

"Why?" I ask.

"Because the sign says so," Will says. "Because it's the law. Because my dad has no idea I have his midlife crisis Escalade in Malibu right now."

I raise my eyebrows. "So?" I ask. "It's Thursday at three P.M. Nobody is here. Nobody is gonna be checking. What's the worst that could happen if they did?"

Slowly, Will nods. Then smiles and nods faster. "You're right," he says. "Cool."

We walk to the trailhead, the Pacific Ocean spreading out in front of us against the horizon. We hike along a steep ridge overlooking the water, and start to wind our way down to a mostly empty beach. Just when we are about to make our final descent, Will stops, and looks out from our little point of land.

"It's really beautiful, isn't it?" I ask him.

"Let's jump." Will turns to me, his eyes wide.

"What?" I ask. "Is that safe?"

Will points to a sign. "Jump at your own risk."

"Exactly," I say.

"If it wasn't safe they'd tell us not to jump at all," he protests.

I think harder. "She probably wouldn't let us die anyway, right?" I ask. "If she's really done with tragedies."

Will thinks. "She does in *Across the Sea*, I suppose."

"But that was different. That was a tragedy, and that death served more of a purpose. To die now would be senseless, foolish. Lucy would never let us do that," I assure him.

"You're really learning a lot in Fiction class," Will says, clearly impressed.

"Thanks." I smile.

"Screw her either way," Will says, and starts pulling off his clothes.

I follow his lead. "I can't believe I'm doing this!" I yell, unhooking my sandals and shimmying out of my shorts.

We stand at the edge in our underwear. "You ready?" he asks.

"I think so," I say.

And we jump.

When we come to the surface a minute later, I feel so energized I could swim for miles. Will whips his hair around and howls like a wolf.

"That was incredible!" he cries.

I laugh and howl, too, and then we are laughing and howling and the sea is whipping around us and the sun is just lowering in the sky. I have never felt so free before. And all with . . . Will?

"This has been a pretty good day," Will says as we crawl out of the water and on to the sand. I'm grateful that none of my undergarments are white, but I also don't really care. I can't help noticing Will's smooth, tan skin, though.

"It has," I say, grinning, wiping salt water off my face. "Thanks to you."

Will stops. "It almost makes me wonder."

"What?" I ask. "If we should skip school more often?"

Will just chuckles, still catching his breath, and lays his head down. "No," he says. "Don't get mad."

"I won't get mad," I promise.

"I wonder if maybe she planned this all along?"

My smile disappears, and I start digging in the sand. I refuse to let her ruin this. I refuse to let the idea of Lucy Keating cloud my judgment, my feelings, my happiness. That was the point of today, after all.

"What do you think?" Will pushes.

"Today has been a good day, Will," I say. "Let's keep it that way."

Will nods, staring up at the sky. "Okay, Annabelle," he agrees.

I look at him for a moment, and then, slowly, I lie down next to him, and lay my head on his chest.

"Do you mind?" I ask, still feeling unsure until I feel his big, warm Will arm come around my shoulder, and his hand rests gently in my hair.

"I don't mind," he says softly, combing his fingers through some of it as we slowly drift into sleep.

22

I'm Sorry You Had to See This

THE NEXT night, I peek my head into my parents' bedroom, where I find my mom reading a book on an Italian architect named Palladio.

"You'd like this guy," she says, pointing to the cover. "He's all about symmetry and simplicity."

"I learned that from you," I say, getting in next to her and curling up on my side.

"Sort of," she says. "I like symmetry, but I'm not necessarily good at it. You got my love of symmetry with your father's intensity. Somehow we created a perfect child."

I wince and stare up at the ceiling.

"What's up?" she asks, folding the book and setting it aside.

"Lately, I don't feel so perfect. Lately, I just feel kind of out of control," I say. "Like I lost my footing somewhere and I can't get it back."

"You're the most in-control person I know," my mom tells me.

"That's part of the problem. I don't really want to be that person anymore," I say. "But I always seem to veer to extremes. I just want to find *myself*."

"Sometimes you have to do something really scary to find yourself," she says, folding one arm behind her head for more support.

"Yesterday I cut school and jumped off a cliff in Malibu. Does that count?" I ask. "And I still feel confused."

Most moms would probably ground me. My mom just nods. "Who did you do that with?" she asks. "Elliot?"

I shake my head. "Will."

"That's surprising. Is he your boyfriend?" she asks.

"He's just a friend," I say. "I think."

"Are you going to Elliot and Sam's show tonight?" my mom asks.

"I haven't decided. . . ." I hesitate.

"Now that Clara's back?" She wrinkles her nose.

I shoot her a look, annoyed at how much she understands everything. "Yes" is all I say. Then I get up and start walking toward the door.

"You know what I think, AB?" my mom says. "I think things change. People change. You don't know what's coming next. I think you have to try your hardest to find your best self, and the person who makes you your best self. I know that better than anyone. Your father and I were that for each other, for a while. But we might not be anymore, and that's what we're trying to figure out."

I pause in the door, listening.

"But I also think you are seventeen years old, and you have a long time before you have to find that person. Right now you have to focus on living your life. On growing. Oftentimes, growing comes after making mistakes. You could do a bit more of that, beyond the cliff jumping."

I walk back over to the bed and lean down and kiss her on the cheek. "Thanks, Mom," I say. "That makes more sense than you know."

I am just standing up when I notice the blanket by her feet move.

"Is that . . . ?" I begin.

Within moments, Napoleon pops his head out.

"I'm sorry you had to see this," she says.

"I thought he hated us all?"

"Like I said, people are capable of change." My mom shrugs. "Even Napoleon. He likes to burrow in by my feet."

Little Boots is one of the only decent places you can see live music on the west side of LA. It's tiny, stifling at times depending on who is playing, which makes it even harder to be shoved in here and watch Elliot and Clara perform together. Luckily, I have Ava and Navid.

"This place is cool," he says, adjusting his glasses and looking happily around the room. "Reminds me of a speakeasy from the nineteen twenties or something."

"He is the dorkiest person you have ever dated," I whisper to Ava when he's not looking. She grins and giddily wraps an arm around his waist. He responds by smiling and leaning down to kiss her on the top of her head.

"So, how do we know these people?" Navid asks.

"Ava's brother is the lead guitarist, and the drummer is—" Ava starts.

"Is nobody," I interrupt her.

Navid throws Ava a look. "So somebody," he says, and Ava shrugs. "I thought you were dating Will?" Navid asks.

"I don't know what I'm doing," I mutter, and just then the lights go dark as Look at Me, Look at Me takes the stage.

Sam is positively radiating happiness as he pulls his guitar over his head. Lenny grabs the bass and picks away a few times, adjusting his amp, and Clara sidles up to the mic. She's wearing a perfectly retro dress and her hair is long on the bottom, but tied up in braids around the top of her head.

And just behind her, face serious and focused, sliding the stool out so he can sit behind the drums, is Elliot.

Elliot looks out into the crowd, and it feels like he's looking right at me. He smiles, and I shiver. Then he raises his arms over his head and counts off as he bangs the sticks together. 1-2-3.

All that practicing in the garage must've paid off, because they sound flawless. Everyone is perfectly in sync, even Clara. I can almost pretend like she's not there, or she's not her. Like I'm not watching the guy I had feelings for and his ex-girlfriend reunite in literal perfect harmony. Instead, I'm just watching a great band play at Little Boots.

Until the last song, when Clara takes the mic.

"Many of you don't know this, but I went away for a little while," she speaks in a smooth, croon-y voice. "I had some thinking to do. But when the tide takes you away, it always brings you back again."

The crowd whistles, and Ava and I share a look. "Pretty sure she stole that from a Folgers Coffee commercial," she says, and I snort.

Clara blushes and whips her hair behind her head. "Anyway, I wrote this when I got back." She glances behind her at Elliot, who watches her skeptically. "I hope you like it," she says.

The beat slows, and Clara gets close to the mic, like she wants to seduce it.

I wandered the desert, I wandered the land
I tried to reach out, to hold on to your hand
I thought I was searching for something more
But somehow I ended up back at your door.

Elliot's face is unreadable as he looks out over the audience, tapping a slow beat, but the one place he's not looking is at Clara. Probably because he feels awkward that I'm here.

And Clara just keeps on going.

Back in your arms, hold me so tight
Tell me you love me, I'll treat you right
You are the one, you'll always be
Perfect, oh, perfect, so perfect for me.

Something overcomes me, and before I can think too much about it, I head straight for the door. I don't want to hear what the next verse says. What it reveals about their perfect love. Why did I come here tonight? I should've known this would happen.

Ava finds me outside, a pitying look on her face.

"Where's Navid?" I ask, my head resting back against the stucco siding of the building, as my eyes stare up at the sky.

"He could tell we needed a sec," she said, and leans a shoulder against the wall, looking at me. "You really like him," she says.

I look at her. "So?" I ask.

"Why is it so hard for you to admit it?" she says.

"Because he's with Clara," I say.

"Don't do that," Ava says. "You have no idea if he is with Clara."

"Because he drives me insane!" I blurt. "And he's all wrong for me. I'm supposed to be with someone like Will. Someone who shows up on time and acts like he wants to be there. Someone who won't hurt me like Elliot can."

"But, Annabelle, I don't show up on time. I'm kind of a mess. And Navid likes me anyway."

"But Navid can trust you with his heart," I say.

Ava frowns. "And why do you think you can't trust Elliot with yours?"

"Because if Elliot isn't sure about anything, how can he be sure about me?" I blurt out.

Ava nods slowly. "I see. That's what you are afraid of," she says. "You're afraid you might fall for him, really fall for him, and you don't feel safe."

I look down at my feet. "It doesn't matter anyway. He has Clara."

"He doesn't have Clara," Ava says. "Listen to me, I'm the one-dimensional sidekick, and I know better. And you're being stupid."

Ava goes to head back inside, and when the door swings open, there is Elliot. My breath stops for a second.

"Hey," he says.

"Oh!" Ava says. "I was just . . . You did a . . ." She pats him on the shoulder as she walks by, then looks back at me open-mouthed and is still giggling when the door swings closed.

"I was just heading off," I say.

"Annabelle," he starts. The door swings open into the club and a pack of girls are there, peering out at Elliot.

"Looks like you have people waiting." I start to turn, and Elliot grabs my arm.

"*Stop!*" he says. "You are driving me nuts. Are you really still this angry at me about what happened at the beach?"

I look at him and want to cry. If he really has to ask, it shows how little it all really meant. I am too afraid to speak right now so I don't say anything.

"Annabelle. Listen, we had a fight. That doesn't mean this has to be over. Fights are something to talk about and work through. But you won't let me. Unless it's more than that. Unless you regret everything that happened. And if that's the case, fine. It sucks, but I can take it. Just don't be weird, okay? I don't like life when you aren't in it."

The door swings open again, and this time Clara peers out.

"You said I was an itch that needed scratching," I manage to say.

"E?" Clara calls as the door swings back shut.

"I was angry." Elliot has never looked more serious in his life. "And . . . I was wrong. I'm so sorry, Annabelle."

The door swings open again and some people exit onto the street.

"Was it for you?" Elliot says. "An itch?"

Just as I am about to open my mouth, a stranger taps Elliot on the shoulder. He's older, around thirty, wearing a leather jacket with a plaid shirt underneath and black jeans.

"Elliot, hey. Great show, man," the guy starts.

"Thanks," Elliot says without looking at him, still waiting for my response.

"Do you have a moment?" the guy asks.

"We just need a minute," Elliot says, still looking at me.

"Of course, my bad." The guy backs off. "I'm Jay Jermaine, by the way. Just wanted to say I'm a big fan."

Elliot's head whips around. "JJ Jermaine? KCRW JJ Jermaine?" he asks.

Jay grins. "Big fan, like I said. I'd love to talk to you when you have a second."

"Your radio show is my life," Elliot whispers.

JJ outright laughs. "Look, I can see you are busy, but I'd love to chat because I just got signed on to do the soundtrack for a big new blockbuster—it's that author Lucy Keating? Not sure if you've heard, but *Across the Sea* is being made into a movie, and they're looking for really original stuff, and I think you guys would be a good fit for at least two tracks."

Elliot looks back at me helplessly, but it's not him I'm mad at now. It's her.

23

Having Fun Yet?

UP UNTIL this point, I think it's fair to say my relationship with Lucy Keating has been complicated. I resented her deeply for butting in to my world, but I also didn't hate her guts.

Now, however, I am going to make her pay.

What kind of sick individual manipulates the life of a perfectly happy teenage girl, and messes it all up for her own professional gain? She wants to give me happiness, she says, but all she is doing is causing me is pain. She continues to create conflict after conflict, giving me low after emotional low, and for what? Just to better her story?

It's almost midnight, and I'm sitting in Sam's car, which I

borrowed despite his protest, in front of Will's house, waiting for him to come outside. I texted him fifteen minutes ago and said to meet me, and as I wait, I let my mind wander briefly to what is probably happening at the club right now. Elliot is surrounded by women, and Clara has her body draped over his. He's probably playing hard to get with her, but their spirits are lifted, happy they're going to license two songs to Lucy's movie. Maybe she'll lean in for a congratulatory hug. And that congratulatory hug will last a moment too long. And as they pull away, foggy and beer-filled, they'll look at each other—

Maybe I am not so bad at creative writing after all, I think, and then lean forward and rest my head against the steering wheel.

The thing is, as long as Lucy Keating is around, there will always be a drumstick or a Clara, an A&R guy, and a broken-down car. I am going to put a stop to this once and for all, and nobody is going to get in my way

"This chick is going down," I say as the passenger door opens and Will's adorable face is there. He looks exhausted.

"What is it?" he asks, rubbing his eyes as he climbs in.

"We're going on an adventure," I say.

"Oh, yeah? Where?" he asks.

"We're going to get to the bottom of this Lucy Keating thing once and for all. We're going to see her in person. Because no matter how much we try to change our own stories, how many cliffs we jump off of or bathrooms we talk in, there's only really one person who can fix it."

"I like it," Will says. "But do we really have to go right now?"

"We have to go now," I say. "There's a chance she's asleep. And if she's asleep, then she can't see us coming."

"Genius," Will breathes. "Can we get coffee first?"

We stop at an all-night diner so Will can get some coffee, and I get a milkshake. It may be one A.M., but I'm so high on adrenaline, I don't need anything else. We are finally going to fix this, I can feel it.

"So, just one more question," Will asks as we buckle up back into the car. "Minor detail, really."

"What's that?" I ask, taking one last gulp of chocolate goodness and setting it in the cup holder, feeling like a superhero who runs on ice cream.

"How exactly do we plan to get there? Did you ask Epstein for her address?" he says.

I shake my head. "There was no time for that, and I didn't want to risk her figuring it out."

"So . . ." Will says.

"So, I'm just going to feel it."

"Annabelle Burns, the most practical person on earth, is going to feel out direction to a destination where she has never been before. . . ." Will does not try to hide his skepticism.

"She made us, Will. I'm her main character. You're her

heartthrob. I can feel this in my bones. I can't tell you the street or the number, but it's in here." I tap my skull. "I just have to follow my instincts."

"Okay, I trust you I guess," Will agrees. "As long as I make it to nine A.M. calculus tomorrow at school."

I wince. "Still working hard at that bad boy thing, huh?" I ask him as I start the ignition.

Will shrugs, taking a sip of coffee. "I am as Lucy made me," he says.

The roads are nice and clear so early in the morning, a miracle by LA standards, and I actually do have a general idea where I'm headed. Somewhere up in Laurel Canyon Lucy is waiting for us. I can feel it. Everything is going according to plan.

But then, just as I'm about to take a right on Sunset Boulevard, waiting for the light to turn green, it turns yellow instead.

"That's weird," I say. "Lights don't go yellow once they turn red."

"It must be broken," Will tells me. "Just go anyway and take it slowly. It's still *proceed with caution*, even if it's not coming after green, and nobody is out here anyway."

But just as I'm inching the car forward, the light changes again. And this time it's blue.

"What the hell?" Will says as I stop the car altogether. "Blue isn't even a color traffic lights *have*."

And then, just like that, the blue flicks to purple. And then it starts flashing like a light show at a roller rink, blinking all the colors of the rainbow. We both take a beat.

"She woke up," I say. Will puts his head in his hands. "And she's torturing us."

"Okay, screw it," Will says, looking up with renewed determination. "She's doing this to us because we play by the rules. She knows we are the only two people who could sit at a multicolored traffic light and *not* just go because it's not green. Prove her wrong, Annabelle," he says.

I hesitate.

"Annabelle!" Will urges me. "You can do this."

And so I do, taking a right onto Melrose beneath the techno lights as Will lets out a cheer.

"But you know what this means," I tell Will.

"What?" he asks, suddenly nervous again.

"It's only going to get harder from here."

And Lucy makes sure of that. We spend four impossible hours detouring all around LA, stopped by everything from construction workers who come out of nowhere to street signs that aren't even the right shape, let alone saying the right thing. One pink stop sign actually says HI THERE, and a sign for the 10 on-ramp just reads HAVING FUN YET?

Eventually, when we go to take Crescent Heights Boulevard

up north up to the Hollywood Hills, the street simply isn't there.

I mean actually, it doesn't exist.

"Okay, no," I say. "That's ridiculous. She cannot just eliminate the existence of geography, of historical landmarks in the city of Los Angeles. She's not that kind of writer. She wouldn't do that to her story."

And, as though somewhere Lucy is stubbornly agreeing with me, the brick wall to my left disappears, and Crescent Heights is right where it's supposed to be, stretching all the way up to the canyons.

Ten minutes later, Will and I are driving through what has to be the longest sunrise humanly possible. I was feeling tired, so he took over. The sky above us has been deep pink for about twenty minutes now.

"She's trying to butter us up," I say from the passenger seat. "Set the stage for romance."

Will keeps driving, a look of calm on his face. He drives beautifully, smoothly, no starts and stops, weaving expertly around other cars. "I'm not complaining," he says. "It's pretty gorgeous."

"Most people think LA sunsets are so pretty because of the smog," I tell him. "But that's actually not the case."

"Explain," Will says as he takes a right onto Fountain Avenue.

"Well, when the sun is high in the sky, we see all the wavelengths evenly—red, orange, yellow, blue, violet. But as the sun moves across the sky, it's farther away, and the atmosphere scatters the blue and violet wavelengths more, so we see more of the red, orange, and yellow."

I glance over at Will and can tell he's listening intently. I like this fact about him. He's not bored and already looking for something else to do. He wants to discuss.

"Anyway, when the sun is setting, it's the farthest distance from the Earth. Blue and violet are scattered almost completely, leaving the warmer tones."

"So what does this have to do with smog?" Will asks.

"People think that the gases in smog scatter the shorter wavelengths even more, creating the pinker sunsets," I say. "The truth is, though, that while natural gases do scatter wavelengths, all our man-made smog does is block everything. So the warm tones you are seeing have nothing to do with us."

When Will doesn't say anything, I look over at him again, worried he's now asleep at the wheel. Instead, he's smiling.

"I'm a nerd," I acknowledge.

"You're awesome," Will says, and he reaches over and rests his hand at the base of my neck. When I tense up under his touch, he removes it.

Will sighs. "Annabelle—"

But he's distracted when the gas light on our dashboard turns on. He rolls his eyes. "You filled this three hours ago," he said. "We've barely used two gallons."

I groan, and roll down the window to yell at the sky. "Do your worst! You can't stop us!" To the right, two little old ladies in a gold Mercedes stare at me.

"Good luck, honey," one of them calls out. "I've been talking to God for years. Hasn't listened yet."

I roll the window up, my eyes wide, and both Will and I start laughing.

"She's right, you know. I have been acting like Lucy Keating is God," I admit.

"She's playing God," Will says. "That's not you; that's all on her."

Once we find a gas station, I decide to run across the street to grab us some bagels at a local deli. I'm just crossing a completely empty street on my way back when I hear Will cry out my name and out of nowhere a scooter is whizzing toward me at full speed, ready to plow me down. Before I know it Will has pulled me from the street and has me wrapped tightly to his chest.

I look up at him slowly, his warmth and cedar smell enveloping me like some kind of drug.

"You okay?" he asks in a low voice, but I pull away.

"We should get going," I tell him, without looking into his gorgeous eyes, and hop back in the car.

We drive in silence for a while, up through the picturesque West Hollywood streets. Suddenly, it's incredibly cold in the car, even though the heat is on. I shiver.

"Want my sweater?" Will asks, pulling it over his head and offering it to me. I stare at it like it's on fire.

"What?" he asks.

"I can't," I say.

"Why not? It's just a sweater, Annabelle, not a wedding ring," he says.

I look out the window for a moment.

"What is it?" Will demands.

"It smells too good," I admit.

I hear Will snort from the passenger seat. "Oh, come on," he says.

I turn and look at him, my face like stone. "I'm serious, Will. It's like a drug seeps out of your pores. It's like opium. I put that thing on and I'm a goner."

"Shut up and put it on, Annabelle," Will says.

Surprised by his tone and freezing to death, I obey. And I'm right. His smell seeps down into my chest. It makes me think of warm fires and Will's shoulders.

"You've never been so firm with me before," I say.

"Maybe I've just been on my best behavior with you," Will says. "Maybe I'm not the nicest guy on earth."

We sit in silence for a moment, and then I say, "Yes, you are."

"Well, I don't always want to be," he says quietly.

"How do you mean?"

"I don't always want to be perfect." He shrugs. "I've tried to screw up before, you know. I won't study for a test, but somehow I'll just know all the answers. I'll sneak out of my house and nobody will even notice. I tried to get a cool old car like Elliot's, not my sensible eco-hybrid crap, and nobody would sell one to me. Sometimes I want to lie or cheat; sometimes I want to punch a guy in the face for being a jerk on the soccer field. But when I go to do it, I just . . . can't."

Something about this strikes me. "Will, I think that means something big," I tell him.

"What do you mean?" he asks.

"It's not new that you want to be more rebellious, or that you're trying," I say, and I can't help think of weird little Napoleon even being capable of change. "But I think it means something that you can acknowledge it like this. That both of us can. I think it must mean we have a shot. Of taking over our own stories. Of not just accepting things as they are."

"I really hope you're right," Will says. "I don't want to live like this forever."

Suddenly, I'm burning up in his sweater, and it feels like it weighs a thousand pounds. I go to pull it off, but despite it being six sizes larger than me, it gets stuck around my head.

"Um, a little help here?" I plead, my voice muffled in the wool.

Around the other side of the fabric, I hear Will chuckle, and the sweater starts to move off my head. But then, for some inexplicable reason, amidst all the twisting and tugging, it seems to get stuck on the other side of *his* head, too. And there we are, trapped at a stop sign in Laurel Canyon, the stars sparkling down at us, the misty back roads on either side, and Will's face is two inches from mine.

"She's doing this," I say quietly.

"I don't care," he says, his voice husky. He leans down toward me, and I breathe him in. And I think how easy this would be, for just a moment. It doesn't have to mean anything. It could just be a kiss.

But then I think about Elliot. What he said outside Little Boots. How that made me feel something more, and swiftly, I pull my head out.

"I think it's just up on the right," I say. And without a word, Will puts the car in drive.

24

Would You Change Anything?

1250 LAUREL Canyon Boulevard sits at a curve in the road, hidden behind a large wooden gate. We ring the bell, but nobody answers.

Will hops up and down a few times to see over the top. "There's a car in the driveway," he says. "She's home; she's just ignoring us."

I lean against the fence, dismayed, and something above us catches my eye.

"When did the stars come out?" I ask. "Shouldn't it be, like, ten A.M.?"

"She's messing with us again," Will says. "Hoping this will

draw us together." He gives me a sidelong glance. I think I must be crazy to have rejected someone as beautiful, as kind, as awesome as Will Hale. But apparently, that's just not how love works.

"Is it just me, or are the stars unusually bright?" I ask.

"You're right, it looks like Christmas tree tinsel up there," Will says, looking up, too. And as soon as he does, a shooting star moves overhead.

"Did you see that?" we both ask each other at the same time. And then we laugh.

Will studies the keypad. "If only we knew the code," he says. "She wouldn't have a choice."

I think hard. "Try her birthday, October tenth," I say, looking at her Wikipedia page on my phone.

"One-oh-one-oh. Nope," Will says.

"Try her birth year, nineteen eighty-four," I say.

"No dice," Will says again after punching a few keys.

"Try MORTY; that's the name of her first dog."

"Morty is not our man," Will says after giving it a shot.

I think for a second. "Try HAPPY," I say.

Will gives me a funny look, but punches it in nonetheless, and magically, the doors open . . . only to reveal another fence.

"Oh come on! This is ridiculous!" I cry. "Now you're just being a child."

At first nothing happens, and then, as though Lucy is once again willing to admit things have gotten out of hand, these doors open begrudgingly, too. Will and I give each other a surprised look, and walk into the compound.

"She wouldn't hurt us, would she?" Will asks suddenly.

"No way. Remember? Then she wouldn't have a book, and this isn't a tragedy," I tell him.

As soon as we enter Lucy's estate, something is off. Over on the right side of the property, a bunch of old cars are piled on top of one another, like they've been discarded in the trash. I recognize every single one from Elliot's dad's shop. But what are they doing here? On another end of the property, Malibu-style cliffs edge around the side, where they don't belong. And now that I look closer at Lucy's house, pieces of it look a lot like mine. And Will's. And Cedar Spring.

As we get closer to the front door, it opens on its own, and Mathilda Forsythe hurries out into the yard, her black portfolio clutched under her arm, her tape recorder in her hand like always. When she sees me, she doesn't look surprised; she just nods and keeps walking out the gate.

"Who is that . . . ?" Will asks.

I watch Mathilda go, my face filled with confusion. "That's the woman who might be buying our house."

"This is so much weirder than I expected," Will mutters as Lucy Keating appears in the doorway of her home. She's in jeans and a black cashmere sweater, three scruffy-looking dogs by her side.

"Annabelle, William." She greets us coolly while beckoning

us inside. "Mathilda was just having a chat about her role. She wanted to talk about whether I could find another place for her in the book. I told her I would think about it. Some characters actually like being told what to do." She puts a hand on her hip.

We move a few steps onto the smooth oak floor of the foyer. Light streams through a giant window on the other side of her living room, over a pile of what looks like the contents of my closet. I can see my favorite ice-blue skirt sitting on top of the pile, and my white Vans sticking out from under the couch.

"Why do you have my clothes?" I ask.

"Honestly, Annabelle, I'm getting tired of explaining all of this to you," Lucy says impatiently. "I'm on a serious dead-line, and I'm already behind. Your clothes are here because I invented them, like I invented you. Everything I think about, everything that's on my mind, is swirling around me in this house. It's just the way it goes."

Lucy does look more stressed than the last time I saw her. Now that I look more closely, her hair is a little greasy, and she has bags under her eyes. I take a little pleasure in it.

"Well, then, I'll make this quick," I say. "We want you to stop doing this."

Lucy tilts her head. "I will also make this quick: no."

"Can you write that smoke is coming out of my ears?" I ask her. "Because it sure feels like it."

Lucy chuckles. "Somehow you are funnier than I ever intended. I didn't know I had it in me."

This only enrages me further.

"See?" Will mutters. "Total God complex."

Lucy rolls her eyes at him.

"Will and I are both here because we want our lives back," I demand. "This is the creepiest, most dysfunctional thing I have ever been a part of, and you should be ashamed of yourself. We want out!"

Lucy looks at Will imploringly. "Is that what you really want, Will? For me to stop writing all of this?"

Will's face has lost a little color. "This is the weirdest moment of my life" is all he says.

"What's your answer?" Lucy pushes, but her tone is still even.

"I want Annabelle," Will admits.

I grit my teeth. He is not helping.

"Well, there you go," Lucy says.

"But I want to know I'm choosing Annabelle because I want to. And that she is choosing me back. And I want to do normal things teenage guys do. I wanna get in trouble for piercing something or tattooing something else. I want to fail an exam. I want to leave my room a mess and not have it magically be all neat again when I get back from the kitchen."

Lucy laughs. "Do you guys hear yourselves? Everything about your lives is perfect. I made it that way. You could have it a lot worse, you know."

"My life is not perfect!" I say. "You are splitting up my parents just to create tension in your stupid book, and I'm spinning out of control. One minute I like Elliot, the next Will. One minute one guy is doing something sweet, another minute he's yelling at me in a lifeguard tower."

"Elliot." Lucy exhales out her nostrils. "He wasn't even supposed to be a main character. He was just supposed to be Sam's annoying friend, comic relief when you were at home. But he kept pushing at his own boundaries."

"Why?" Will asks.

"Because Elliot isn't the right guy for her," Lucy says. "You are."

At this, Will's eyes widen.

"How do you know?" I nearly yell. I've never felt so misunderstood in my life. I've never felt so . . . trapped.

"Because I know, trust me," she says. "Elliot is not your guy. Elliot isn't even in control of his own life. A character like Elliot . . ." Lucy pauses and sighs. "Annabelle, he only breaks your heart."

Now this stops me for a moment, because it's the first thing Lucy has said or done that might be true to my understanding of life. Because if I'm being honest, I've always had a suspicion he would.

Lucy takes a step closer. "Trust me, Annabelle. I know what I'm talking about. Trust someone who once chose the wrong guy. Your story with Elliot does not end well."

My heart is clenching in my chest, and I look down at my shoes. "Maybe it will," I try.

"No." Lucy shakes her head. "Listen to yourself. You don't even think it will. And I'm here to tell you it doesn't. Let me give you the Happy Ending you deserve."

Behind Lucy, I watch Napoleon wander out from the kitchen, look at me, and hop up onto the couch. Patio lights from Sea Salt Creamery are strung around the hallway. Cookies from the Malibu Country Mart are on a plate on the coffee table, and I think my father's surfboard is leaning against the refrigerator.

"Love isn't supposed to be hard, Annabelle," Lucy says.

"Since when?" I ask.

"Let me give you the correct ending," she says again.

"How do you know what that even is?" I demand.

"Because I created you," she says without pausing.

"Total God complex," Will repeats.

"Oh, shut *up*, Will," Lucy says in exasperation.

"Elliot is what I want," I say, because I mean it. I feel it deep within me. I turn to Will. "Will, you really are perfect. For me and even in general. You are honestly everything I thought I wanted that didn't exist. Someone is going to be very lucky to be with you."

Will smiles, but it's a sad smile.

Now I turn my attention back to Lucy. "I didn't pick Elliot. One day it just smacked me across the head. But you don't get to pick the people you fall in love with. You know this better than anyone. You don't get to choose for me."

I glance around Lucy's house some more, before noticing

that the names of all my friends and family are written on a whiteboard above her desk. These names, once just a word written in marker, are real people to me. Their lives mean something.

I think about my parents, and tears come to my eyes. "And just because something ends, doesn't mean it didn't mean anything. Sometimes, you have to take the risk."

Lucy has gone still, and she stares at me, continuing to absently scratch her dog's head.

"If you had a chance to do it over," I say. "Would you?"

"Do what over?" Lucy asks suspiciously.

"Do it over with Edwin," I say.

Lucy looks at me sharply. "How do you know about that?" she asks.

"It doesn't matter. Would you really do it differently? Would you take it all back, even if you were only going to grow apart in the end?" I ask her.

Lucy sets her dog down, and wraps her arms tightly around her torso. "Losing him was the most painful experience of my life," she says softly.

"But would you change anything?" I press her.

Lucy swallows, then seems to snap out of it.

"You guys need to go," she says. "Now."

"We aren't leaving until you agree to let us decide things for ourselves," I say stubbornly, because I think I have nearly cracked her.

"Fine!" Lucy exclaims. "If that's what you want, Annabelle, that's what you're going to get." She marches toward her front door, and holds it open for us.

"Wait a minute," Will says, his eyes worried.

"Good!" I yell back, walking out the door.

"Hang on," Will cautions.

"If that's what you want, Annabelle, I'm going to stop writing your life." Lucy shrugs, watching us from her doorway.

"Why does this suddenly seem like a bad idea?" Will asks, following me back out the gate.

"Let's go, Will," I say, grabbing him by the arm and pulling him along more quickly, back across the front yard that has waves crashing against the garden wall.

"See how you like it!" is the last thing I hear Lucy call before the gate shuts.

25

In the Drawer

AS WE make our way toward home, winding down Laurel Canyon and through the west side of LA, it's as though a giant weight has been lifted off my shoulders. I haven't felt this light in weeks, since before Lucy showed up. The path before me feels clear. My decisions are finally my own, and nobody is going to get in my way.

So it takes me a little while to notice that Will is completely silent. He stares straight ahead, but the light from his eyes is gone, his face expressionless.

"I'm sorry, Will," I finally say as we turn off of Venice

Boulevard onto my street. "But I meant what I said. And you do deserve better."

"There is no better than you, in my mind," he says, as though he's given up. "I feel hopeless. Like a werewolf in *Twilight* who has imprinted on someone."

I snort. "You've been reading *Twilight*?" I ask.

"You think I wouldn't do my research?" Will says. "I watched the movie. Did people really freak out that much about that series? Jacob is the obvious choice. Edward is so . . . serious."

I bite my lip, trying not to smile.

"What?" Will frowns. "What's so funny?"

"I hate to break it to you, but in this book, in the scenario Lucy Keating created . . . you are Edward."

"No . . ." Will starts. "Because you are choosing Elliot, so that makes me Jacob."

"No." I shake my head with a pitying look. "In Lucy's conception, you are Edward, and Elliot is Jacob. He's not even Jacob status, really. But you are the one I'm supposedly destined for."

"Well, now I'm Jacob, though, right? In this reality?" Will looks at me a little desperately.

I pat him gently on the arm. "Yes. Now you can be Jacob."

Will seems satisfied with this.

As we pull up outside my house, and I go to remove my hand from Will's arm, I notice that it looks strange. It's weirdly fuzzy, like I'm looking at it through a piece of warped glass. I rub my eyes, blink, and look again, but it doesn't help. There's no depth, no shadow. My whole hand appears flat, like it's made of paper. Will notices it, too.

"Will. What happening?" I say, holding my hand out to look at it more closely. There are no knuckles, no wrinkle creases where my hand meets my wrist. My throat catches in my chest when I realize that suddenly there aren't even any fingernails.

"Oh, no," Will says, a panicked look on his face. "This is exactly what I was afraid of. But I didn't know it would happen like this."

"Afraid of what?" The edges of my hands are starting to fade and lose their pigment.

"You look . . . like a comic book character," Will tells me. "You're, like, two-dimensional. Like Animal Man." And when I look up at him I see what he means, because so is he. His hair looks like it's painted and would be stiff to the touch, and his eyes are large circles in the middle of his face. And when he turns to the side, he all but disappears. It's like I'm sitting next to a paper doll.

Outside the car, all around us, the world seems to be getting brighter, like someone is editing a photo of us on their phone and pushing exposure to the highest level. I shield my eyes with one hand.

"Why is everything disappearing?" I cry out, but my voice comes out muffled.

"She stopped writing us, Annabelle," Will says, looking around, and his voice sounds farther away than it should. "Our world is ceasing to exist, and we are going to go with it."

"It's not disappearing. We can't just disap—" I start to tell him, but when I turn to Will, he's gone, and so is the car we were just sitting in. Only a bleached-out street corner remains. I rotate back around again, and where The House should be, it looks like a life-size rendering of my mom's exterior house elevations. Just an outline of my childhood home, as though drawn in pen, set against a bright white backdrop. It sends a wave of fear rushing through me. I run to the front door, throwing it open.

"Mom? Dad? Sam?" I call out, but on the other side of the doorframe, there is nothing but whiteness. I think I hear voices from far away, but I can't see anything. Then the voices fade to nothing. Now, there isn't even the outline of a house. Everything is gone.

I take a few steps in one direction, then start to run full speed in another for what feels like twenty minutes but could be three. It's so hard to tell anything when there is nothing to use as a frame of reference. I keep hoping to see something in the distance, for a speck of the familiar to come into view, but nothing changes. It's just blank.

Unsure of where else to go or what to do, I sit down on the white surface. It's not hard like the floor of a house would be, but it's not soft, either. It's smooth and matte, like I'm sitting on top of a piece of my mom's vellum paper. I wrap my arms around my knees, and try to think. My heart is beating quickly, and my brain feels fuzzy. I can't seem to hold on to any of my thoughts.

I take a deep breath, attempting to regain some focus. "Try, Annabelle," I urge myself. "You can do this."

I close my eyes, rocking back and forth, struggling to hang on to something, and then I hear Elliot's voice, even more crackly than usual. It's like I'm listening to a recording of him from our fight on the beach through a long-distance phone line. He's telling me that maybe I like being written, so I have an excuse for when things aren't going according to my plan, for when I lose control.

"It's not true," I whisper. "I don't want that anymore." An image of him appears in my head, like a worn-out photograph, standing outside Little Boots as he asked me to tell him what was happening between us. I am disappearing, and the last thing I think is that I will never get to tell Elliot how I really feel.

And then another image replaces it, and I see Lucy standing in front of me in the school parking lot, that very first day.

"Some of my characters demand to be heard," I hear her say, leaning against the side of her car. "Others just sit in a drawer, waiting for the right time."

I lay my forehead against my knees, realizing that my world isn't simply ceasing to exist, I am going "into the drawer," like a piece of discarded manuscript. Who knows how long I could stay in here, waiting for Lucy to decide I'm worth it after all. Now I understand her choice of words back at her house. *See how you like it*, she'd said. She knew this was where I was going as soon as we walked out the door. She said she'd stop writing, but she was never really going to set us free.

"I am not going in a drawer," I protest quietly, using the last of my strength. "I am trying to write my story."

I sit up, unwrapping my arms from my legs, and when I rest a hand on the ground, it hits something hard and cool to the touch.

It's a pen. A thick, glossy ballpoint pen. I pick it up carefully, holding it in front of my face to examine it. The weight of it feels good in my hand.

And that's when I think about Ava. How she said that it was the ambiguity that scared me. That I should embrace it, and take it slow. I lay my head down and close my eyes, and I begin to think through everything I've been so afraid of. What will happen if I don't keep my Sunday schedule? What will happen if I choose to give myself to Elliot? What will happen when I come home next year, to a different house, with only one parent in it?

And what I begin to realize, slowly, is that while a lot will happen, while none of it will be easy, none of it will mean the end of anything, or the end of me. Because I am Annabelle, and I will always know who I am, even if I'm not always sure what I really want.

But right now, I do know what I want. What I want is Elliot Apfel.

All I want to do is sleep, but I know I can't. Not yet. I just keep thinking about Elliot, how good it feels to be with him, about how it felt that night on the bikes, riding through Venice beneath the streetlights, how it felt to be curled up on the lifeguard tower, wrapped in his arms. That, right there, is exactly where I want to be.

I drag myself back up so my legs are tucked under me, and uncap the pen. Then I use one hand for support as I lean over my knees. I press the pen gently down on the white surface that extends before me, enjoying how it feels as the pen glides, leaving ink marks in its wake. And then I begin to write.

I have the power now.

And slowly, the scene that I put on paper begins to take shape. Out of the white, as though appearing from the mist, I hear the waves of Venice Beach crashing and seagulls overhead, and I feel the sand of the beach beneath me. The outline of the water rippling to shore appears ahead, and coming out of the waves, a board under his arm, pushing his hair back from his face, is Elliot.

26

I Am Elliot, and You Are Annabelle

"LET ME see if I have this right," Elliot says. We're back at the lifeguard tower, nestled up with some blankets. It's been almost an hour since he appeared out of the white nothing-ness, which dissolved into an ocean mist, and so far, nothing has gone wrong. In fact, everything couldn't be more right. I can feel it, deep down in some basic part of me—I am free from her. I wonder where Will is, and if he knows this yet, too. I wonder if he's tried to run a red light or leave a problem set unfinished for the morning, and discovered he actually could. I wonder if he knows he gets to decide his own fate now. I'll have to text him later, but right now I'm busy.

Elliot's head is leaning back against the wood, and I have my chin resting on his shoulder. He's frowning as he lets a hand absently stroke the top of my head. "So you really figured out that this chick Lucy Keating was writing your life?"

"Yes," I say.

"And she was writing you to be with Will."

"Yes." I nod.

"Not me," he says.

"Not you." I shake my head.

"Well, why the hell *not*?" he yells. "Thanks a lot, Lisa Keating, or whatever your name is."

I giggle, not even bothering to correct him. I'm pretty sure he did it on purpose anyway.

"So you drove all the way to Laurel Canyon to defend how you feel for me?" he asks.

I shrug. "I mean, also to fight for my own free will, but yes," I say. Elliot kisses my forehead.

"I'm really glad you did," he says.

I feel truly happy. Calm. I'm not worried about what's next on my schedule or what I have to plan for. Right now just about anything could happen and I won't mind. I'm with Elliot, and that's how it should be. To be honest, I'm not even sure what day it is.

"But really, can we go back to me for a second? What did I do that was so very wrong? So very unworthy of Annabelle Bellybutton Burns?" Elliot whines.

"I think—" I swallow, trying to find the words. "I think she wasn't sure if you were right for me."

Elliot tips his head to the side, eyeing me. "She didn't, or you didn't?"

I sigh. "Elliot. My whole life you have been everywhere, but you have never been with me. I've seen girl after girl sit in that garage drooling during band practice. And then there was Clara. And I've never dated anyone. Ever. And we're not exactly compatible. And when you did pursue me, you didn't seem that sure about it yourself."

Elliot shifts and starts to get up, and I feel scared. I said too much. I should've played it cooler.

But all he does is kneel on both his knees and stare into my face.

"Annabelle. I have always been with *you*. Even if it took me a little while to realize it. I've been in your garage. I've been on your stupid couch every chance I get. I've been in your kitchen every time I could convince your brother to let me stay for dinner. Do you think I do that for anyone else?"

I shrug. "Yeah, sort of," I admit. Then I chuckle.

Elliot laughs. "No," he says. "Annabelle, you are more real to me than any character I've ever read. Than any other person I've ever met. I like that you say things that you mean. That you say things out loud sometimes that you probably shouldn't. That you're interested in everything and know weird facts that nobody else takes the time to consider. Screw Lucy's plan and screw her useless, contrived love stories. I am Elliot and you are Annabelle. Maybe I wasn't fated to be with you, but it doesn't stop how crazy about you I am."

I knew being honest with Elliot about how I felt would feel good, but I'm not sure I ever knew he was capable of saying stuff like this to *me*. I wanted this before I even knew I wanted this. Elliot on my couch, bugging me when I'm trying to do my homework. Elliot skating by me at school, pulling my hair. Elliot banging away on the drums like nothing else on earth matters.

"But what about next year?" I ask.

Elliot sighs. "I don't know about next year, Annbelle. We're just getting started. What I know is that I want to be with you every moment of every day right *now*. I know that I want you in my story." He leans down and grasps my chin in his hand.

"But what about the day you wake up and you don't want that anymore? What if I don't? What then?"

Elliot looks deeply into my eyes. "You can't go through life always worrying about what is ten steps ahead. You can't expect anything real or awesome to happen to you, if you don't take a chance." Elliot holds my gaze, waiting.

I nod. "I want you in my story, too," I say, and then Elliot leans in and kisses me.

That night, I lie in my bed thinking about everything that happened over the past twenty-four hours. About how I almost lost it all, even myself. But how I fought for it, and how much I've gained because I did.

Most surprisingly, I realize that I might actually understand Lucy Keating better than I ever thought I could. Because now that I know what love is, now that I know I might be able to hold it close, I understand just how painful it would be to lose it. I don't blame her for wanting to change things for me. If I look deep inside myself, I wonder if I might have done the same thing.

My phone buzzes under Napoleon's butt, and he growls in his sleep. This is the first time he's ever slept in my bed, and I'm just going to let it happen.

The text is from Elliot, and it's a song. The same one he sent me when we were fighting, that I never listened to. This time I press PLAY.

I know I've heard this song before, but I guess I've never really listened. The most beautiful strumming hits my ears first for the intro, followed by the first verse and chorus, Van Morrison singing the words "sweet thing" over and over. This is a true love song.

AB: I like this.

EA: It reminds me of you.

I put a hand in front of my face, glad he can't see me blushing. And then come these words:

And I shall drive my chariot down your streets and cry
"Hey it's me, I'm Dynamite, and I don't know why"

I know what he means, because right now I feel this way, too. Like I could jump the hedges and run screaming through the streets, yelling that everything is awesome, because it is. Because I have Elliot.

EA: Let's listen together.

AB: How?

The next thing I know, there is a small crack against my window. I go look out and Elliot is standing on my front lawn, throwing pebbles.

"What are you doing?" I ask.

"Is this romantic enough for you?" he whisper-shouts, opening his arms wide. I am grateful, for once, that my dad is sleeping in his lair, and my mom sleeps like a rock. Suddenly, it starts to rain.

"Where did you learn how to do this?" I whisper back.

"I was pissed that Lucy didn't think I was enough. I Googled classic teen romance. A lot of stuff from the eighties comes up," he says. "Now let me in. I'm soaking wet, and I want to listen to 'Sweet Thing' with you."

I nod my head with a smile, and Elliot uses the first-floor

porch and a drain pipe to help him climb up the side of the house.

After he hauls his body through the window of my bedroom, we stare at each other for a moment. This is happening. I realize I'm shaking a little bit, and I've never been more nervous. I love it and hate it at the same time.

"You're wet," I say, and go to grab a towel from the bathroom. When I get back, Elliot's shirt is off. I pause in the doorway.

"Is this okay?" he asks.

"Yup," I squeak. *Keep it cool, AB,* I say to myself. I walk toward him with the towel, and like a pony ready to have his mane combed, he leans his soggy, wild head of hair toward me.

Laughing softly, I put the towel over his head, rubbing against his skull. Then I pull it down around his shoulders, and continue to gently dry his limbs. Every cell in my body is whirring around and around, and I haven't met his eyes. When I do, they are half closed, but they are watching me.

"Hey, Annabelle," he says.

"Hey, Elliot," I say and swallow.

And then he takes the towel out of my hands and lets it drop on the floor. And he puts his hands on my face and kisses me.

We kiss and kiss and kiss, and end up tangled on the sofa.

"I've been trying to get you on this couch with me for years," Elliot's crackly voice says, and I flick his shoulder playfully.

"You had a funny way of showing it," I say. I'm on top of

him, staring down at his face, and let my fingers trace along his hairline. When they reach his ears, he purrs.

"I was working the long game," he says simply, and I start giggling. We both laugh, and Elliot shifts so I am facing him, tucked into his chest. And his breath starts to come more evenly.

We lie there, curled up into each other. The notes from "Sweet Thing," which I put on repeat, crash over us in waves as violins join the rhythm of the guitar. I don't know if this makes sense, but this song sounds like falling in love.

"It's perfect," I say, letting my whole body relax. I rest my head against him and I think, *This is not a sure thing.* There are no promises here. But I'm seventeen years old, and the only place in the world I wanna be is on this couch, with this guy, listening to this song over and over again. And maybe tomorrow it will all be different. But I don't care.

27

Thanks for Being a Part of My Story

"**WAKE UP,** Annabelle," someone says. I open my eyes to find Sam standing above my bed, his wetsuit draped over one arm. I can't see much, but I can see that it's barely light out.

"What do you want?" I grumble.

"You're graduating high school today. So we're going surfing," he tells me. "Right now."

"What time is it?" I ask.

"Six A.M."

"What if I don't feel like it?" I ask.

"That's exactly why we need to go," he says, stepping back to take a look around my room. Clothes, books, and other kinds of junk cover every surface. "What the hell is going on in here anyway?"

"Like you should talk," I argue, sitting up in bed. "Your room looks this bad *after* you clean it."

"Yeah, that's me we are talking about," Sam says, picking up a few empty cans of Diet Coke and tossing them in the trash.

"Maybe I'm trying something new." I shrug.

"Well, stop," Sam says. "It's gross."

I stay where I am, looking at him stubbornly.

"Don't make me carry you out," Sam says. "You know I will."

The problem is, he absolutely will. So with an eye roll, I heave myself out of bed to put on my swimsuit.

As we head for the beach, the sun coming up, I lean my head back against the seat of my brother's car and close my eyes.

"If you're doing this because Mom and Dad asked you to," I say, "you really needn't bother."

"I'm not," Sam says, his eyes on the road.

"Well, if you're doing this so you can talk to me about Elliot, or the divorce, just don't," I say eventually. It's hard to get the words out. This is unfamiliar territory for us, and also, I really don't feel like talking about it.

"Wasn't planning on talking about Elliot" is all Sam says. "Just wanna take my little sister surfing like the good old days."

I told my whole family about me and Elliot a few days ago

over breakfast. I did it with a lot of dramatic flair. I even got the Good Coffees. To be honest, I was looking forward to shocking them. But to my great disappointment, my parents just smiled, and Sam shrugged as he wolfed down his scrambled eggs. He wasn't thrilled about it, but he wasn't exactly surprised, either.

The beach is nearly empty this morning, and only a few other people are out on the waves. The sun is fully over the horizon now and lighting up our part of the world. We spend nearly two gorgeous hours out there. Every muscle in my body feels ready to call it quits, but I'm having way too much fun.

When I paddle back out after riding a wave all the way to shore, Sam is watching me, a strange look on his face as he straddles his board.

"Oh, boy," I say. I know that look. He's about to say something serious.

"Hear me out," Sam says. "I'll make it quick."

I roll my eyes, but I listen.

Sam takes a deep breath. "You know I'd never let anything happen to you, right?"

I make a face. "When? Out here? Sam, I haven't been afraid of sharks since the fourth grade, but thanks anyway."

Sam shakes his head. "Out here, back there." He points to shore. "What I'm trying to say, AB, is that just because Mom and Dad are splitting up, doesn't mean you are all alone. I'm your big brother. It's my job to watch out for you."

Suddenly, I feel like I am going to cry. Not just because my brother's never really said anything like this to me before, or because it helps to know he has my back. But because for the first time, in this moment, I can acknowledge how scared I really feel. I had assumed, though I never said so out loud, that when Lucy stopped writing my life, my parents would magically be back together. Like it was all just a bad dream. But that's not what happened. My dad is still sleeping in the guest house, and my mom is still going through the motions, clearly a little fragile, trying to take it all one day at a time. Maybe in the same way that Elliot fought through his story to be with me, my parents really did want to get a divorce.

"But what if you can't be," I say. "What if you go off on tour or something, and I have to come home at Thanksgiving and spend it with just Mom or Dad, all alone. That will be awful."

"That's not going to happen," Sam says.

"How do you know?" I ask. I wipe away a tear, grateful that we are both already soaking wet.

"Because Mom and Dad are weird, so they will probably always spend it together regardless, but even if they don't, I will always be here. Wherever I am in the world, I will come back."

I stare at my board. "Do you promise?"

"I promise, AB. Swear on Napoleon's life."

I sniff, and let out a giggle. My brother is watching me with a twisted smile, his eyes sad.

"Well, I promise, too," I say, and smile back through my tears.

When we arrive back at The House, my dad is just taking the general out on a walk. "You two have a good time?" he asks us.

"She killed it," Sam says, unloading the boards. "She's getting really good, Dad."

"Better than her old man?" my dad asks.

"She's gaining on you for sure," Sam tells him.

"Hey, AB," my dad calls when he reaches the fence, Napoleon trotting behind. "Something was on the front steps when I came outside this morning. An envelope. I put it on your bed."

"Thanks, Dad," I say as I go to hang up my wetsuit to dry.

"And, Annabelle?" my dad calls again.

"Yeah?" I ask.

"I never thought I'd ever have to say this to you, but for God's sake, clean your room," he says sternly. Then he smiles.

I walk into my bedroom with renewed energy and get right down to business, throwing all my clothes into one pile, trash into the bin, and stacking books on top of my desk. It's only when I move to straighten my bed that I see the envelope lying on top of the covers, and handwriting I've come to know all too well scrawled across the front.

Miss Annabelle Burns: 732 Oakwood Avenue, Venice, CA

Feeling my breath start to come more quickly, I rip off the envelope, and a letter falls out, on her signature blue stationary: FROM THE DESK OF LUCY HARRISON KEATING.

Annabelle,

I want to tell you that I'm sorry for many things. I'm sorry for taking over your life. I'm sorry for not listening to you when you asked me to stop. I'm sorry for letting my own heartache seep into your world. But mostly, I'm sorry about what I did to you and Elliot. I know you love him.

On that topic, I can tell you two things. One, he loves you back—trust me. And two, your relationship was real. I didn't create that one. Elliot was merely a side character, but he fought his way into your story to be with you.

And you: You are a brilliant character, AB, but I'm afraid I can't take all the credit. You may have been my creation, but you were always you. This is who you are, like it or not.

The end is up to you now, Annabelle. You'll find your Happy Ending, and it's not about with whom you end up. I am only just beginning to figure that out.

Until next time,
Lucy Keating

I take a moment to sit on my bed, staring at the letter in front of me. An apology from Lucy Keating? I never thought she was capable of such a thing.

But, more important, she's right. Elliot and I did fight to be together, and what we have is real.

And, most significantly of all: I love him.

Public speaking is not something I've ever had a particular problem with. I've seen people melt down over even the prospect of standing up in front of strangers, and others hold a carefully written speech with shaking hands. But to me, like so many things in life, it's something you simply do when you are asked to do it. What could being nervous practically accomplish?

The question on my mind now, as I stand before my classmates, teachers, friends, and family, as the valedictorian of Cedar Spring's graduating senior class, is what I should choose to do with this moment. It probably isn't a surprising fact to learn that I've had my speech written since the beginning of the year. I planned to reference Diane Sawyer, her brilliance and determination, and her advice to young people like me to always "Aim High."

But as I look down at my carefully written note cards, something isn't sitting right with me. And when I open my mouth to speak, I talk about a different woman in history. Someone that nobody expected, least of all myself.

"Those who know me are well aware that I've been thinking about my future practically since birth." I smile at the crowd, and a low murmur of laughter reaches my ears. "Since a very young age, a big part of that future has always involved being a journalist. I love to explore stories in current events and even history, and unearth their greater meaning in our world.

"Earlier this year, I stumbled upon the story of what has come to be known as the Egtved Girl," I say, looking out over the audience. "The Egtved Girl's burial place was uncovered in the nineteen twenties in a moss-covered area of Denmark. She was a teenager at the time of her death, but at the time of her exhumation, she was nearly four thousand years old."

I let that number settle over the crowd, before I continue.

"Scholars were able to determine that the girl was on the shorter side, about five feet three inches, and she wore a surprisingly modern outfit: what was essentially a miniskirt and T-shirt made out of wool. Her hair, they could tell, had been short and blonde. In other words, what I realized was that the Egtved Girl looked a whole lot like *me*."

As I anticipated, the audience enjoys this comparison.

"Over the last month, I've found myself thinking about this girl. When they first dug her up, historians assumed she was native to the area. But nearly one hundred years later, scientists were able to determine through analysis of her fingernails and fibers in her clothing, as well as other things buried along with her, that she had traveled great distances. Possibly on foot, possibly by boat, possibly a little of both. I wondered, What had her life really been like? And dying so young, what had it all meant? In four thousand years, if the Earth is still here, what will people say about me?"

I swallow, choosing my next words carefully.

"I guess the message I want to send to my classmates is this: We often feel quite a bit of pressure on our shoulders, and sometimes we don't even realize it's there. So I'd like to offer you this advice—don't be afraid to surprise yourselves. People thought they had the Egtved Girl all figured out. They thought she was probably a local teen who had never seen very much in the world. In actuality, it turns out she had seen a great deal. She might have even been someone really important. Maybe she'd been someone who'd made great change in her very short life.

"My plans are still intact," I say. "I still intend to head to Columbia in the fall and pursue a career in journalism. I don't do this because it was my plan; it was my plan because I love it. But I'm determined not to stick to it too closely. I have no idea what surprises the future will hold. Now my plan is to follow my dreams. My plan is to surprise myself, and write my own story. I hope, whatever age you are, each one of you chooses to do the same. Thank you."

I step away from the podium while the audience erupts in deafening cheers, and as I make my way back to my seat, there's only one person I don't see clapping. It's Elliot. He's watching me, and he's grinning.

I am just shoving a brownie into my mouth, my graduation cap tucked under one arm, when I bump straight into Ruth Epstein.

"I could not be prouder," she says, clasping her hands together, her bracelets jangling.

"Really?" I ask her.

"Really," Epstein says. "What a brilliant, unexpected story to tell." She shakes her head. "You are going to make a great journalist someday, Annabelle Burns."

"That means a lot to me, Miss Epstein," I say, giving her a hug.

"And great job on your final project, too," she whispers in my ear as she holds me tightly. "Grades aren't due for another week, but you nailed it. How you ever came up with a crazy story about a character and her author waging war on each other is beyond me, but you blew my mind."

I hug her tighter. She doesn't need to know that I made very little up at all. That once again, I was retelling a story that already existed. But honestly, I don't really care. You can't be perfect at everything. Sometimes you just have to do your best. And a small part of me enjoys the fact that after everything Lucy did, I flipped it on itself and used it to my advantage in the end.

"Annabelle, hey," I hear a familiar voice say, and turn to find Will waiting patiently. "You were awesome," he says.

"Thanks, Will," I say, and after the silence between us lasts one moment too long, I ask. "So, what's new?" When I got to-gether with Elliot, we both decided it would be best to take a little space so Will could figure out who he was, and what he actually wanted.

"Well"—Will leans in, his smile turning mischievous—"check this out." He raises the bottom of his pristine collared shirt, and up underneath his shoulder blade is a tattoo. It's small, but it definitely makes an impact.

"It's Hawaiian," he tells me excitedly. "I found it in an old album passed down in the family. I went into the shop and nobody even stopped me. It was exhilarating!"

"That's amazing!" I say, and give him a big hug.

"So are you excited for New York in the fall?" Will asks.

"I can't wait," I say. "Where will you be?"

"Actually"—Will looks down at his feet, blushing—"looks like we won't be too far away from each other. I got off the waitlist at Yale a few days ago."

"Will, that's *amazing*," I say. "Congrats. Maybe I'll see you in the city sometime."

"I'd really like that," Will says sincerely. "Who knows? Maybe we'll find ourselves in the same story again someday, Annabelle." And with the ever-dazzling Will Hale grin, he heads off to hug his mother. I watch him go for a moment, and then I run up to him.

"Hey," I say, grabbing him by the shoulder. Will spins around.

"What?" he asks.

"I guess . . . I just wanted to say thanks," I say.

"For what?" Will looks equal parts delighted and confused.

"For being a part of my story," I tell him. "I couldn't have done it without you."

"Yes, you could have." Will tilts his head.

"Okay, maybe I could have," I say. "But it was a lot more fun with you in it."

"Get your butt to my house in thirty minutes, or we are leaving for Palm Springs without you!" Ava yells into the phone. Behind her, I hear Lee squealing.

"What's going on over there?" I ask, throwing my cap and gown down on my bed. "Why are you guys always yelling?"

"We aren't telling you until you get here!" Ava yells louder. I'm just telling her I'll be right over when I realize she's already hung up the phone. We're headed to the desert for a celebratory weekend, just us girls. We've had it planned since December. I'm so excited I almost want to go without packing.

It's for this reason that it takes me a solid minute and a half to notice Elliot lying on my couch, staring at the ceiling.

"Oh. Hi," I say.

"Hope it's okay that I'm here," he says. "Your mom let me in."

"Of course it's okay," I tell him, like he's crazy, but I still haven't gone over to him yet.

"You're being weird," he observes. "You haven't been returning all of my texts. I know you do that when you've got a problem you can't figure out how to solve."

I nod. "I know," I admit. Because I have.

"Your speech . . ." he starts.

"Unexpected?" I ask.

"Awesome," he says. He sits up and runs a hand through his hair. "You never cease to surprise me, Bellybutton."

I hesitate, shifting from one foot to the other, but can't stop myself from moving over to the couch. Without saying a word, I wrap my arms around his waist and his arms come around my shoulders, and we lay back, curled around each other.

I let out a long sigh. "I'm scared."

"I know," Elliot says.

"What if we don't make it?" I ask.

Elliot rests his chin on the top of my head. "I want to tell you that we will, but we both know I can't do that," he says. "This isn't one of Lisa Keating's books anymore."

I giggle into his neck. Elliot refuses to call Lucy Keating anything other than Lisa. Ever. It's his way of fighting back, his own micro-aggression against how she treated us. I think it's hilarious.

"You could come with me?" I say. "To New York."

"I could," Elliot says, giving me a brief glimpse of hope. "I might, someday. But not right now. Look at Me, Look at Me have made a name for ourselves in LA. It would be a mistake to pick up and move now."

"But," I start, "what if you meet some hot girl at a party one night, and unlike me, she *can* play an instrument, like really well? And you like her more than you like me?" These are the things I've been thinking about. The things that have been keeping me awake at night lately.

"That's not going to happen." Elliot shakes his head.

"What if I have, like, the sexiest resident advisor on the entire campus of Columbia, and he's basically a prince of a small country, and he starts hanging around all the time and—"

"First of all," Elliot interrupts me, "never give me that hypothetical situation again. Second of all, there are changes coming our way. We both know that, and we know we can't avoid them. I don't know what is going to happen to us, but I just know that I cannot lose you."

I close my eyes, because he's right. I don't want to be vulnerable. But then I tell myself that just this once, it might be okay to let go.

"I don't want to lose you, either," I admit.

"I know it sounds crazy," Elliot confesses, "but I just want to know I can come and sit on this couch. This couch is important to me." I can hear his heart beating.

"This couch is important to me, too," I say even though we both know we're not really talking about the couch. The couch won't even be here soon. We keep holding each other, my head in Elliot's neck. "Sweet Thing" isn't playing anywhere—if Lucy were writing this, it would be—but I play the violins in my head.

"I love you, Annabelle," Elliot says, and then he tilts his head down to look at me, and I trace the freckles around his eyes with my fingers, like always. We kiss.

After a few minutes, I say, "You'll always be my first love, Elliot. Though given that I've never really dated anyone else, I suppose it's not saying much."

Elliot is quiet for a moment. "You'll always be my first love, too," he says. "And, speaking as someone who has dated quite a few people, I can tell you that it means a whole lot."

28

That's Not What the Word Means

IT'S THREE P.M. on Tuesday afternoon, and technically I should be in Freshman English at Columbia. That's what my calendar says, in blue. But I'm not. Instead I'm standing backstage at Warner Bros., on the set of *Across the Sea*, watching Elliot get a final makeup touch-up before they start shooting.

Yes, as in the film adaptation of *Across the Sea*, by Lucy Keating.

In the end, JJ Jermaine pulled through for one of his biggest fans, and Look at Me, Look at Me didn't just get chosen for the soundtrack of *Across the Sea*, they got chosen to perform live as the band in the movie's sentimental prom scene. Clara has on a poufy taffeta dress and all the boys are wearing ice-blue tuxedos with ruffled cummerbunds. They should look ridiculous, but they actually look kind of awesome. Particularly Elliot. He catches my eye as the pink makeup sponge dots its way across his cheekbones, and winks. I smile and stare down at my shoes. After all this time, he still makes me nervous.

"Don't cover up all his freckles," I tell the makeup artist, who rolls her eyes at me.

Elliot invited me to set for this big moment, and I decided to fly out for a couple of days. This doesn't mean I'm not taking school or my future seriously. That's a part of my DNA. But I've learned to live a little. To shake things up, as my dad would say. And plus, I could ace Freshman English with my eyes closed, so I'm not too worried about it.

I feel my stomach grumble, and I head over to craft services to see if there are any chocolate chip cookies I can dig up. That's when I bump headfirst into Diane Sawyer coming around a corner. She's in black slacks and her signature collared shirt, and she looks incredible, as always.

"Pardon me!" Diane says, putting a hand to her chest like she's just seen a ghost, before disappearing down the hall. I'm left standing there, my mouth hanging open, all the things I've always wanted to say to her running through my mind on repeat.

"A little starstruck?" a PA wearing a headset asks as she walks by.

"I'm her biggest fan," I whisper.

The PA stops. "Aren't you a little young to be a fan of Diane?" She winks.

"What is she doing here?" I ask, choosing this time to ignore the joke.

"She's interviewing Lucy Keating. She's the author who wrote—"

"I know who she is," I say curtly.

The PA nods. "Well, she's on set today, and Diane was in town for some awards ceremony. They decided to shoot the interview here. If you go quickly, you might be able to catch some of it."

I hesitate, not wanting to miss Sam and Elliot's big moment.

"Go," Elliot says, coming up behind me and giving me a kiss on the cheek before reaching for a bagel. "We aren't shooting for another hour anyway."

"I love you," I tell him. And then I start to run.

⸻

"It's an honor to host you on our show today," Diane Sawyer tells her guest. "Congrats on the success of *Across the Sea*. Everyone is very excited for the movie. I think I may have used up an entire box of tissues when I read the book."

"It's a pleasure to be here, Diane," Lucy Keating says, looking beautiful and confident in a chic gray blouse and her signature red lipstick. Her glasses are new, I notice. Now they're tortoise-shell.

"Before we get into the film, I know everyone in the audience has one question on their minds: Are you working on anything new?" Diane crosses her legs elegantly, letting one hand rest gingerly in her lap. *Books could be written on her composure*, I think.

"I've got a project in the works," Lucy says. "I can't really talk about it yet, but I can say that I'm aging up a bit. This one takes place in college."

A familiar, prickly feeling starts to meander up my spine.

"How exciting!" Diane exclaims. "Will there be romance?"

Lucy smirks.

I roll my eyes. Next to me, a girl walks by, talking loudly into her cell phone. "He was literally the hottest guy I've ever seen," she says, and I want to tell her that's not actually what the word means, but stop myself. Our entire generation is misusing it anyway. What's the harm in living outside the lines?

Acknowledgments

My editors: Sara Shandler, Hayley Wagreich, Jocelyn Davies—this book is as much yours as it is mine. Thank you for seeing me through this process and approaching every draft with true enthusiasm, no matter how much our heads were hurting. I learn from each and every note you make on the page, even when I fight you on it at first (particularly when I haven't had my coffee yet—sorry about that).

My thought partners: Josh Bank, you weirdo, for having a dream where I kidnapped one of my characters, the impetus for this whole crazy thing. Joelle Hobeika for, as usual, wrangling us all back to Earth.

My agent: Pete Knapp, for coming onto the scene and making everything better, when all I could give him in return was ice cream. And, of course, for introducing me to Louis the Dog, Napoleon's kindred spirit.

My roomie: Zana Lawrence, for sharing my wall, and for reminding me that we're all just doing our best.

My parents: Marty and Mike, for telling me that sometimes, you know what? It's okay to turn something in late.

My family unit: Mom, Dad, Mike, Andy, Shannon, Laura, for never making me feel bad about spending holidays at the library, instead of where I really wanted to be—watching movies on the couch with you.

My friends: You know who you are. For your forgiveness, your wisdom, your unconditional love.

Dave Ferino: for introducing me to Animal Man!

My first high school English teacher: Meredith Price, who made Andover feel like so much less of a scary place.

My heartthrobs: the ones who've made me smile and made me cry, the ones who've showed up in tuxedos on Valentine's Day, the ones who never got on the plane, and the ones who did.

And Ernie Bear: The sweetest, tiniest beast of all.

Also by Lucy Keating

Lucy Keating

DREAMOLOGY

The boy of her dreams just might be real.

HARPER TEEN

An *Imprint* of HarperCollins*Publishers*

www.epicreads.com

JOIN THE Epic Reads COMMUNITY

THE ULTIMATE YA DESTINATION

◀ **DISCOVER** ▶
your next favorite read

◀ **MEET** ▶
new authors to love

◀ **WIN** ▶
free books

◀ **SHARE** ▶
infographics, playlists, quizzes, and more

◀ **WATCH** ▶
the latest videos

www.epicreads.com